NIAGARA FALLS
INTO DARKNESS

FRANK THOMAS CROISDALE

Cataract City Publishing

ASIN: B087N3RRK4
ISBN: 9798640066081

Cover design by: Art Painter
Library of Congress Control Number: 2018675309
Printed in the United States of America

For my two sons, Zach and Ryan. I'm so very proud to be your Dad.

To Maureen, my everything. Your love has redeemed my soul. Being your husband is the greatest honor I could ever know.

PRAISE FOR *NIAGARA FALLS INTO DARKNESS*

"Dean Koontz, John Grisham, James Patterson - make way for the next great American crime thriller author, Frank Thomas Croisdale. Not only is *Niagara Falls Into Darkness* a page-turning masterpiece, it features one of the greatest protagonists ever created for the written page."

-Mick O'Malley, *Niagara Falls Insider*

"If you have money left over after tipping me and you plan on buying a book, buy mine. Then buy 'Niagara Falls Into Darkness', it's the real skinny on just what lies beneath this town's shiny neon exterior. It's got everything: Chilling true crime exploits, sex, a mystery that will have you scratching your head raw, sex, and even a history lesson or two. Did I mention sex?"

-Robert "The Hook" Hookey, *The Bellman Chronicles*

"Despite my utter disdain for Mick O'Malley I just couldn't put *Niagara Falls Into Darkness* down. It's an instant classic."

-Jeffery Lordes, *Niagara Falls Morning News*

"I know a rising trend when I smell one. Mark it down: *Niagara Falls Into Darkness* is the next great thing in modern literature. In *Law,* Croisdale has created a villain who will haunt your dreams for days after you finish the final chapter."

-Chickie Crossvalley, *Niagara Falls Insider*

CHAPTER 1

May 25th

People are always amazed by sleight of hand because they keep their eyes on the wand and not on the magician thought the man that the world would soon know by the monosyllabic moniker "Law." *An exaggerated hand movement here, an unnecessary flourish there and presto, a rabbit is seemingly pulled from thin air - all to the astonishment of a group of slack-jawed simpletons clapping wildly as if they'd just seen the second coming of Jesus Christ himself.*

Today, I'll show them some magic, thought Law as the hint of a smile teased from the corners of his mouth. *I'll make the lady in the box disappear and even the great Harry Houdini himself couldn't bring her back.*

Law had these thoughts as he was looking through a coin operated pair of observation binoculars high atop the Skylon Tower in Niagara Falls, Ontario. Everyone else in the burgeoning Memorial Day weekend crowd had their eyes on the main attraction – world famous Niagara Falls. Law was glad that they had come to see the wondrous cataracts even if he wasn't thrilled with their chosen vantage point.

Every idiot and his offspring from America's heartland can't wait to get up in the tower or on the Niagara Falls boat ride while wholly ignoring the natural views of the falls provided from Goat Island. Just another example of people praying at the altar of science and technology while turning a blind eye to the majestic work of God.

Just then a buzz came over the crowd as, literally, a buzz went over them from above. A helicopter carrying Hollywood leading lady Lauren Tate came into view and made the first of five scheduled passes in front of Niagara Falls.

My lady in the box thought Law.

Tate was in town to shoot a scene for her new movie "Barrel Queen." The film would tell the tale of the first person to purposely go over the falls, Annie Edson Taylor. Taylor, who was a 63-year old schoolteacher when she made her plunge in 1901, was responsible for setting off the "daredevil explosion" that still raged at Niagara. The movie promised to usher in a new genre – that of historical/action adventure.

Along with Tate and the pilot, there was a studio cameraman on board shooting footage of the scene below to be used in the movie's after credit scenes.

Like most modern movies shot at Niagara Falls, little of the final footage would actually be captured on the banks of the Niagara River. Most would be shot on a Hollywood film stage with a few true on-location shots thrown in for good measure. If necessary, an additional scene of falls footage could be added in during post-production just by having Tate and her co-star, Bryce Hunter, stand in front of a green screen back in Tinseltown. The helicopter fly-over wouldn't be part of the film, but the producers knew that it would be shown on everything from CNN to Entertainment Tonight and would be the first step in a calculated and expensive marketing campaign to make sure that theater seats would be full on the movie's opening weekend.

Law watched as the helicopter made its second pass and stole a glance at his watch just as a Chinese mother standing next to him was struggling with the pronunciation of Lauren Tate's name as she attempted to explain to her pre-kindergartner what all the fuss was about.

11:58 AM was the read-out on Law's gold-plated digital watch. *2 minutes until the rabbit comes out of the hat.*

The crowd seemed to be peaking with excitement as the helicopter came in for the third pass. The rainbow adorned tourist helicopter carrying Tate was closely flanked by one from CNN and another from ABC News. The ground beneath the Skylon was filled with satellite towers flying flags from outlets ranging from local news stations to the BBC.

Good, thought Law, *let them all bear witness to my warning. While their eyes were centered on the diversion of the falls, I set them up for the grand finale. While they were looking at the wand they didn't even notice that they were in the presence of the grand magician.*

Just then the digital display on Law's watch blipped to 12:00 and the helicopter carrying Lauren Tate exploded in a fiery blast. As hundreds of thousands of tourists watched in person and millions more gazed on in horror in front of their televisions, Hollywood lost one of its top leading women and Niagara Falls, the tourist destination, lost its innocence.

Men could be heard screaming and women and children were shrieking and crying. News crews below scrambled to cover what would be the biggest story of the summer. Everyone in the Skylon was in a state of panic wondering if the terrorism they'd just witnessed would be limited to just the helicopter or was the tower coming down, too.

Against this backdrop, Law lit an unfiltered Camel cigarette and did something for the first time in months.

He laughed.

CHAPTER 2

I put the telephone back in the cradle and let out a long, slow whistle.

"What was that all about," asked Johnny Gutenzarro, Johnny "Guts" to his friends and enemies alike.

"It was Sally over at Homicide, all hell's broken loose. Lauren Tate was killed this afternoon. Her helicopter blew up and they don't think it was an accident."

"No shit. No fucking shit," Johnny Guts said. "I'll get Howard right over there for some pics."

My name is Mick O'Malley. I'm 35, but on days when the sunlight is kind I can easily pass for a man still in his 20s. My full head of dark hair has never hurt me when it came to wooing the ladies. Neither too has my 6'2" height, 185 gym-sculpted pounds, piercing blue eyes and gift for gab. At least that's the way my mother tells it to the ladies in her Words With Friends circle.

I'm Editor in Chief of the *Niagara Falls Insider*, a weekly tabloid newspaper that has a reputation for holding public officials up by their ankles before kicking them squarely in the balls.

Johnny Guts is the publisher of the paper, one that he and I dreamt up one night 6 years earlier over too many rounds of Crown Royal and Cokes at Rumrunner Ray's. Somehow sobriety the next morning hadn't tempered our enthusiasm and we convinced a consortium of investors to pony up a grand apiece as seed money to get the venture off of the ground.

We had little idea on how to actually run a newspaper and that turned out to be a good thing. We hit the ground running with the idea that we'd fake it until we could make it. It was a lot of trial and error, but we were quick learners fueled by an endless supply of piss and vinegar.

The daily paper in Niagara Falls, the *Morning News*, called the *Insider* "pure folly" and gave us 6 months at best before going belly up. Now, some 300 issues and hundreds of thousands of lost advertising dollars later, the *Morning News* considers the *Insider* a pest on the verge of becoming a locust and wished like hell they'd never sacked me from my city hall beat some 7 years ago. I don't exactly wish them peace and love either.

"Tell Howard to try and get a shot of the wreckage. The *News* would never run it, but we sure as hell can," I said as Johnny Guts had already hit the speed dial button on his cell phone for the Insider's ace photographer.

"Johnny, there's more. Sally said they found a note. It was from Law. I think it's time I told her about the emails"

Johnny Guts stood stunned with his mouth hanging open as, from his cellphone, Howard Dodson's voice could be heard repeatedly yelling "Hello."

CHAPTER 3

I looked up from my peanut stick doughnut as Sally Wendt walked tiredly through the front door of Frankie's – the best doughnut and coffee shop in Niagara Falls.

"Sorry it took me so long to get here. The Feds are crawling all over the Tate murder like carpenter ants on a dropped popsicle," Wendt said as she sidled into the booth across from me. "What's up? You said you have something for me?"

"Yeah, Sal. You mentioned on the phone that you found a note from someone named Law. Well, I think you need to take a look at these."

I handed the plucky 5'4", 32 year-old, redheaded detective a stack of emails each consisting of one or two line warnings. Every one of them was signed "Law."

"Holy shit, Mick. How long have you been holding out on me with these?"

"Oh, come on Sal. I get fifteen crackpot emails like these every day. If I called you every time some nutcase made a threat you'd have to put a cot in my office. Not that I'd object to seeing you in a nightie, mind you. I just figured this guy was another frustrated loser living in his mama's basement with access to the internet."

"He may be," Sally replied, her cheeks flush with blood as the result of the compliment I had tossed her way, "but he's a loser who has killed one of Hollywood's biggest stars now. The FBI has over a dozen agents on the case and we've got every cop in town pulling doubles to get the investigation jump started."

Sally leafed through the half-dozen sheets of paper I'd given her. Her brow furrowed intoxicatingly as she read and reread each one two or three times before speaking. As she concentrated my eyes wandered down her curvy body, then back up again for good measure. Even in a detective's conservative clothes her sensuality shown through. There was strong sexual tension between us, had been for years. But Sal was married to Craig, her high school sweetheart; they had two kids, a dog, a cat and a nice house in the DeVeaux section of town. In short, the American Dream and as a result our relationship was relegated to that of friends with flirting benefits.

"This is some crazy shit, Mick. This guy's got a lot of anger issues," Sally said as a waitress came over and took her order of a cup of green tea and a bran muffin.

"This is the first one then, the one dated March 11th?" Sally asked as her order was placed in front of her.

"Yeah, they came spaced apart about every two weeks or so, up until the last one 8 days ago on the 19th," I said as I dunked my peanut stick doughnut into my coffee with double, double.

Sal read the first correspondence from Law out loud.

"Niagara Falls has flowed for centuries, soon Niagara Falls into darkness."

"Nice play on words," I offered, but Sal's mind was already racing forward.

"The second one, dated the 26th, says, 'They call Clifton Hill the 'Street of Fun,' but the fun has not yet begun.'"

Clifton Hill is the strip in Niagara Falls, Ontario filled with wax museums and souvenir shops. It is often the first thing cited by folks when arguing against the commercialization of Niagara.

Sally flipped through the next three emails and stopped and stared hard at the last one sent.

"This is adding up bad Mick, real bad. This is one evil dude."

I choked down the last of my doughnut as she read the final email.

"The Devil's Hole Massacre will look like a tea party compared to what I'm about to do. The Niagara River will run red with blood – and it's on the hands of all of you."

The Devil's Hole Massacre took place on the lower Niagara River in September of 1763. A wagon train traveling between Fort Schlosser and Fort Niagara was beset upon by a group of 300 or more Seneca Indians. The terrain along that part of the Niagara Gorge is steep and narrow. The horses in the wagon train broke into stampede and went over the rocks to their deaths taking men, women and children along with them. A detachment from the British 18th Regiment was dispatched to rescue the wagon train. They, too, were attacked by the Seneca warriors. By the time the sun sat in the Western night sky 102 people were dead. It still remains as the single bloodiest day in the history of Niagara Falls.

"That's some threat," I offered.

"That's just it Mick, my gut tells me we're not dealing with threats here as much as we are promises. I'll run a trace on his IP addy and let you know what we find. Promise me you'll let me know right away if he writes again."

"I promise, on one condition: I need a quote from the lead detective for my column."

"You want a quote Mick? Here it is: 'Niagara may have fallen into darkness with the murder of Lauren Tate this morning, but we're going to shine a light until whomever is responsible is brought to justice.' And if you don't like that, make the shit up yourself"

CHAPTER 4

Law carefully extinguished his cigarette with the heel of his shoe and bent over to pick up the butt before depositing it in the trash can at the entrance of Three Sisters Islands. *No one should desecrate such a wondrous temple of God's beauty by littering* thought Law just as a fat tourist sporting a tie-dyed Ole Miss T-shirt tossed an ice cream cone wrapper onto the ground mere feet from the waste can. Law thought about taking out his survival knife and vivisecting the bloated ignoramus on the spot, but settled for a just slightly less combative solution.

"Where do you think you are, some Southern hootenanny? Pick that up and place it in the can or I'll snap your fingers like dry twigs," Law barked in a voice so commanding that the smattering of tourists milling about within earshot all came to a sudden halt.

The tourist, who'd never met a buffet he could resist, sized up Law and decided that compliance was his best retort. He scooped up the wrapper and put it in the waste can.

"Sorry, Man. No disrespect intended."

"You're about to enter Three Sisters Islands, respect is a requirement," Law said. "And for God's sake, if not mine, tuck in that hideous shirt of yours."

Law loved Three Sisters above all locations surrounding Niagara Falls. The islands, flanking the south side of the larger Goat Island, are named after the daughters of General Parkhurst Whitney – Asenath, Angelina and Celinda-Eliza. General Whitney was a prominent early settler of Niagara Falls, New York. He relocated to the city in 1810 and is best remembered as the proprietor of the famed Cataract House Hotel, which employed an all-black wait staff and was a major stop on the Underground Railroad.

The islands are connected by a series of footbridges and all feature paths that lead to various views of the upper rapids where many tourists have been tempted to slip off their shoes and dip their feet in the cool running water. Three Sisters is as natural as Niagara comes these days and the fact that most tourists never find it, and pollute it with their presence, made Law happy indeed.

Reaching the third island, Celinda-Eliza, Law stood atop the large flat rock marking the center spot and took in an unmatched view of the upper rapids. Some 700,000 gallons of water per second was rushing by. Law noted that the water intake valves just a few hundred yards east were diverting a nearly equal number of gallons. That water would travel in underground tunnels to the hydro power plant down river where it would cascade down turbines and create electricity. Law took solace in the green energy technology made possible by Niagara Falls, but lamented the fact that the Falls, as God intended them to be experienced, were a thing of the past.

From his vantage point Law took out a pair of binoculars and could have easily passed for just another visitor from Dubuque, Boise, Omaha or any other Midwest outpost. However, the magnified view in Law's eyes was not that of rushing water, but of towering steel. His gaze was intent upon the Strata-Screamer ride at AquaticWorld across the river in Niagara Falls, Ontario.

AquaticWorld is a park with an identity problem. It doesn't know if it wants to be a theme park or an aquarium. Built in the early '60s it is definitely old school as far as theme parks are concerned. The Strata-Screamer is billed as "the world's highest triple tower ride." Constructed on a 150-ft. high hill the ride jacks seated, harnessed riders up another 230-ft before dropping them screaming and pissing themselves toward the ground below.

Many riders of the Strata-Screamer marvel at the view of the falls from the ride's apex. Those glowing reviews turned Law's stomach. To compare the majestic view of Niagara with the thrills of a cheap, carnival ride was an injustice unforgivable in his mind. Today they will pay for their insolence.

As he peered through his binoculars, Law enjoyed the sweet caw of a chickadee circling one of the many maple trees to call Celinda-Eliza home. As the bird flew across to an unattached fourth island, known as Little Brother, an explosion lit up the early evening sky brighter than the fireworks common each evening at 10 PM during the tourism season. The Strata-Screamer, which had just ascended with a half-full load of tourism industry officials taking a FAM tour of the park, went up like a Roman candle as cries of disbelief rose on both sides of the river.

Finally lived up to its name, thought Law. And as assorted body parts rained down over the holding pools of AquaticWorld he mused, "Well, they won't have to feed the killer whales today."

CHAPTER 5

I sat in the fifth row of a half-packed auditorium at the main library and tried my damndest not to fall asleep. There were two things working against my quest to remain awake: the fact that since the AquaticWorld and Tate killings I'd slept a total of about four hours over three days and the incredibly dry lecture being given about the need to return the lower Niagara to a Greenway state.

The lecturer was one of my old college professors, John Brintkowski. Back when I was an English major at Niagara University, Prof. B taught a class on the Romantic poets that I had surprisingly enjoyed so much I received an "A." I could still see him standing in front of the class, his silver-speckled hair shining in the late afternoon sun, as he passionately read one of my favorite lines from Shelley:

"Oh! lift me as a wave, a leaf, a cloud!
I fall upon the thorns of life! I bleed!"

Since his retirement five years ago Prof. B sat on more boards then a room full of ceramics. His greatest passion was reserved for the Greenway Project. The movement's objective was to create a progression of nature along the waterfront between lakes Erie and Ontario. The Niagara Falls contingent, of whom Prof. B was the unelected spokesman, wanted to tear up the four-lane concrete Robert Moses Parkway and return the land to God's good glory. Following what they called the "Olmstead Vision" the Green Freaks, as Johnny Guts referred to them whenever he was sure there wasn't a microphone running, sought to restore all of the natural fauna surrounding the falls.

I honestly couldn't give a shit one way or the other. All I cared about was filling my newspaper with advertisers and making enough scratch to one day retire from the glamorous life of endless deadlines. I turned up for these snooze fests solely out of allegiance to the man who had taught me the power contained within rhyming couplets, but I still had a hell of a time feigning plausible interest in the subject matter.

Just as my head jerked back for the hundredth time I was saved by the sweet smell of a certain redheaded cop's perfume.

"I see Brintkowski is still as boring as the missionary position," said Sally as she slid into an empty seat directly behind me.

"Yeah, with the lights off. Hey, is that Eternity?"

"Yes. You know it's scary that you know shit like that. Most guys are lucky if they even notice when you've gotten your hair cut let alone what type of perfume you're wearing."

"I'm just gifted I guess. What brings you out to the lecture circuit?" I asked.

"I'm here to spring your candy ass. We received a message from Law."

"You did?" I said as I whirled in my seat to face her, wide awake now. "What did he say?"

"He sent an email, same IP address as his emails to you. He used a burner phone so there's no way to trace them. He said that you had all of the answers to our questions at your office. Mick, are you holding out on me again?"

"No, Sal. I was there until lunch and then hit the streets trying to figure out who the fucker is. Johnny's in Buffalo trying to work the feds for info, so the place has been locked up most of the day."

"Come on perfume Kreskin, my car's double parked outside, let's get a move on."

It took Sal just a few minutes to get us over to the Insider's offices on the 2nd floor of the trendy Niagara Office Center. It didn't take long to decipher Law's message. A thick Manila envelope had been slid under the door and I nearly tripped over it as we entered the darkened offices.

I flipped on a light and picked up the envelope. The words: "For Mick O'Malley's Eyes Only" was stenciled out in black block letters on the envelope front. I undid the clasp and reached in and pulled out 25 typed pages that had been bound with a combed spine complete with plastic front and back covers.

"What is it?" Sally asked.

I turned to look straight into her emerald green peepers, "It's his manifesto."

CHAPTER 6

Sally pulled a pair of plastic gloves from her purse and slipped them on to examine the manifesto without smearing any fingerprints Law may have left behind.

"You and Craig playing groped by the gyno again?"

"I wish. Actually we're in a bit of a sex slump. Try to keep your one-track mind on the job at hand, Mick," Sally said while carefully opening the manifesto to page one and reading it aloud.

Laws have been broken – my laws. New laws will now be enforced – also my laws. There is but one sheriff, one judge, one jury – me. Adhere to my demands and you will live to a ripe old age. Defy me and pay with what you least can afford to part with – your life. What follows are the things that you need to begin, or stop, doing if you want my reign of terror to end. By now you surely know that I am a man of action, one not to be trifled with.

"Not much of an egomaniac is he?" I offered.

"Jesus, there's twenty-four long-winded pages of his rules. Does he really think that we're going to digest all of this and then snap into lock step?" Sally asked while beginning to take down notes on a yellow legal pad.

"Hey, that's familiar," I said as Sal stopped at the paragraph I was pointing to on page 4.

You cannot be disciplined in great things and undisciplined in small things. Brave undisciplined men have no chance against the discipline and valor of other men. Have you ever seen a few policemen han-

NIAGARA FALLS INTO DARKNESS

dle a crowd?

"It's a quote from Patton when he addressed the men of the Second Armored Division," I said.

"This one seems familiar too, Mick. I can't remember where I heard it. Do you recognize it?" Sally asked before reading the passage on page 8 aloud.

I'm not going to change the way I look or the way I feel to conform to anything. I've always been a freak. So I've been a freak all my life and I have to live with that, you know. I'm one of those people.

"Yeah, it's John Lennon. It's from one of the last interviews he did before he was shot. Sal, I think that the whole thing is nothing but quotes from other people. That one there," I pointed to a paragraph on page 15," is the philosopher Kant. *'Act that your principle of action might safely be made a law for the whole world,'* and this one here is Mark Twain, *'Loyalty to the country always. Loyalty to the government when it deserves it.'*"

"Why would he do that, Sal?"

"Profilers. He knows that the FBI profilers will dissect this thing seven ways from Sunday and put together an all-too-accurate for his liking composite of who he is. Age, race, profession, religion, social status – you name it. The Fibbies could probably even tell if he hangs his Johnson on the left or the right, but by making his point with other people's words all they'll know for sure is that he's well-read."

"Yeah, that and the fact that it looks like I'm his boy," I said pointing to the final sentence on page twenty-five.

I will communicate through Mick O'Malley and Mick O'Malley only.

CHAPTER 7

After two hours of dissection and Internet checking Sally and I attributed the quotes in the manifesto to twelve different people. They were, in alphabetical order: Cheever (John), Ginsberg (Allen), Kant (Immanuel), Kennedy (John), Lennon (John), Lincoln (Abraham), Patton (George), Roosevelt (Teddy), Simpson (Homer), Steinbeck (John), Twain (Mark) and Updike (John).

"That's some list, Mick. What does it tell you?"

"Aside from the fact that nearly half of them are named John and most are dead white guys, I think it tells me that this guy wanted to give us one big cluster fuck that we could never unwind."

"I think you're right. The Homer Simpson quote gives it all away."

"Let's see, here it is: 'The lesson is: Our God is vengeful! O spiteful one, show me who to smite and they shall be smoten.' Why is that his reveal, Sal?"

"Because everyone who quotes the Simpsons always has a funny line, like: 'Now, thanks to the Internet, even sex is boring.' The quote he obviously Googled was just to bolster his promise of death and destruction. He probably didn't even realize he was quoting a fucking cartoon."

"What's the move now?" I asked.

"I'm going to turn this over to Carlson, the lead FBI agent, and see what forensics can come up with. He's such an arrogant prick – I'd rather eat broken glass. I've been a respected cop in this town for twelve years waiting for a case like this and then boom, these clowns roll in and take over the whole ball of wax."

"When will I get it back so that I can run it in the paper?"

"Mick, you can't run word one until you get FBI clearance."

"I'm quite sure that a little thing known as the First Amendment to the Constitution says I can."

"If you piss off Carlson, he'll make your life miserable. It's a battle you don't want, Mick."

"Sal, I've got an idea that can help us both. Get Carlson on the phone for me."

Five minutes later I was on speaker phone with a very agitated FBI Senior Special Agent Keith Carlson. Sally had briefed him on the manifesto and he was quite pissed at hearing about it hours later than he felt he should have.

"Make this quick, O'Malley. You're already in hot water for withholding evidence from the federal government."

"I must respectfully disagree, Agent Carlson. The manifesto was delivered to me at my place of business and I have constitutional rights to both its possession and its publication."

"If you try to print one word of that madman's ramblings, I'll have a court injunction shutting down your entire publication."

"I've got Western New York's best trial lawyer on a big retainer for just such an emergency. Plus, you try to shut down one newspaper and you ensure that you'll be on the front page of all the others."

"What do you propose then O'Malley?"

I swallowed hard and gave Sally a wink.

"Well, how about a solution that works for both of us. First, I turn over the manifesto to you immediately. When you're done checking it for fingerprints and trace evidence you copy it and send me a copy. In 72 hours I print it, in its entirety, in the *Insider*. Until then you promise not to leak it to any other newspapers or media outlets. I furthermore agree to turn over all future correspondences from Law as soon as I receive them."

"Is that it, Mr. O'Malley?"

"Yes. Well, except for one small point. Law says he'll only communicate with me. I want to only communicate with Detective Wendt. I know her, I trust her and she'll take whatever information I get straight to you. Deal?"

I held my breath; Sal looked like she wanted to faint.

"Done," was the only word Carlson spoke before hanging up the phone.

Sally, maybe still in shock over essentially being put in charge of the investigation, stared hard into my eyes. Then she did something that I never saw coming – she kissed me full on the lips.

"Sometimes I love you more than life itself, Mick O'Malley."

CHAPTER 8

June 1st

I spent the better part of the next morning churning out three stories for the Insider. Because we're a weekly I have the liberty of writing long – around 1,200 to 1,500 words a pop, more magazine length than the standard 800-word newspaper allotment.

The three pieces I was working on – an expose of a city councilman's failure to pay taxes on an apartment unit on the city's north end, a commentary on the lack of funding in the city budget for pothole repair and an interview I'd done with a rape victim who claimed that the cops responding to her 911 call treated her like a perp because of her job as an exotic dancer – all deserved full write-ups, but were getting shortchanged due to the Law manifesto.

I gave a bare-bones effort for each and gleefully hit the "save" icon in my Microsoft Word tool bar. I'd planned the seventy-two hours I'd asked Carlson for just perfectly to fit the print deadline for the *Insider.* We hit the streets each Wednesday afternoon. Full content had to be sent to the news press in Buffalo by noon Tuesday. So long as there were no snags all of Niagara Falls would be reading the words of a madman as they enjoyed their midweek lunch. Normally, we posted the online edition on Tuesday night. Not this week, however. I didn't want all of the national news outlets to steal our thunder and plaster the manifesto all over the airwaves before our hardcopy went out. By dinnertime on Wednesday the whole country would be watching breaking news shots of television reporters holding up copies of the *Niagara Falls Insider.* For the cover I'd chosen a picture of a shadowy figure that vaguely resembled the Unabomber. The headline would scream: The Long Arm of the Law: A Mass-Murderer Speaks.

I looked at my watch and saw that it was 12:30. My growling stomach let me know that I'd been neglecting too many meals over the past few days. I decided to head over to Rumrunner Ray's for a bite to eat and to catch up with a certain waitress by the name of Sara.

Sara Evans was 23 and beautiful in the way that only young women are. She was tall and didn't have an extra pound hiding anywhere on her sultry body. Her blue eyes could melt a rattler's cold heart and her big tits could make his tail wag like that of a Collie. She was also my girlfriend.

Girlfriend is the wrong word – too strong for me and too casual for her. She was hoping to become Mrs. Mick O'Malley while I was looking for a sexual partner with girlfriend benefits.

I'd met Sara at a political fundraiser two years ago. She had graduated from Niagara University with a degree in Travel and Tourism and the depressed economy forced her to put that education to use as a waitress in a rundown tavern. She'd seen my byline in the paper and mistook me for some sort of a local celebrity. Newspaper groupies are rare, but not unheard of. Usually they look more like Jessica Tandy than Jessica Alba though, so when she went fishing I bit quick and hard.

Sara has a small apartment on the 3rd floor of a 100-year old house overlooking the Niagara River on Buffalo Avenue about a quarter mile from the *Insider's* offices. That makes it convenient for me to pop in and fuck her brains out once or twice a week. I'd like to say that we make love, but lying isn't one of my character flaws. Sara was abused as a child and it manifests itself in a twisted sex drive. She likes to be submissive in bed. I've handcuffed her to the posts, spanked her ass red and called her names that would make the most hardened streetwalker blush – all of which left Niagara Falls as the second wettest thing in town.

Truth be told I'd enjoyed these sexual perversions at first, but now found them exhausting. I know I'll come off sounding like a chick, but what's wrong with kissing and cuddling once in awhile?

I'd intended to end things with Sara for some time, but the lure of easy sex always tempers my wanderlust. Once the police nailed Law was my new timeframe, replacing once we'd gotten back from our weekend in the Poconos and before that, once Valentine's Day had passed.

"Hey, Daddy, your little girl's been missing you. It's about time you came to see me," Sara purred while pouring me a coke with no ice.

"Yeah, babe, I've missed you too, but this Law bullsh…" was all I got out as a response before Sara bent down and shoved her tongue down my throat.

"Damn, girl. Get a room," said Roxy the barmaid, as she rolled her eyes at a scene that shamelessly she'd seen a dozen or more times before when I'd visited Ray's.

Rumrunner Ray's was part of a bar scene in Niagara Falls that never made the press releases put out by the tourism council. The city was rife with corner dives where, as the old song goes, everybody knows your name. Short on ambiance and long on cheap drinks and eats, Ray's is a place where you can get yourself and your date fed and drunk for under $40 – a price tag that fit both my budget and Sara's libido.

I ordered a Beef on Weck – a Western New York staple and Ray's specialty. The sandwich features thinly sliced roast beef with gravy served on a hard roll topped with kimmelweck seeds and coarse salt. Many people topped the sandwich with horseradish, but I found enough bitterness in the world and always took mine straight up. I also ordered a side of chunky bleu cheese dressing to dip my accompanying french fries in – also a local tradition.

"So is my big, strong handsome Daddy going to catch that big, bad Law before he can hurt anybody else?" Sara asked.

Except it came out in one long blurt, void of breaths between words. It was one of a list of things that I detested about Sara outside of the sack – she always talked like the elevator door was closing.

"I'll leave the catching business to the professionals – Sally and the FBI. I'm just getting his manifesto ready for the paper. I've got about an hour's worth of work left on my commentary, which I will finish tonight."

Sara turned her nose up at the mention of Sal. She tolerated our friendship, but made no bones about the fact that she considered Sally Wendt a rival and trusted her no further than she could spit.

Just then Bobby the cook rang the bell signaling that my order was ready. Sara sashayed her pretty backside over to the counter and sat the sandwich and fries down in front of me.

"Here you go Daddy. Enjoy."

Sara then leaned over and whispered in my ear, "Make sure you come by when you're done tonight. I've been a naughty girl and I need to get punished."

CHAPTER 9

Law stared at the shriveled shrunken head behind the display case glass and wanted to vomit. For all intents and purposes to anyone paying attention he would easily pass as just another tourist taking in the over-the-top entertainment scene along Clifton Hill.

Of all places surrounding Niagara Falls, Law hated the "Street of Fun" more than any other. Every aspect of it – the honky-tonk glitz, the mega-decibels of noise and the pagan-like worship of demonic scenes and rituals – infuriated him with a rage that he found difficult to contain.

Just 30 minutes ago, while he stood face-to-face with an actor portraying Freddie Kruger inside of the Primal Fear Museum, Law had to suppress the urge to pull out his concealed hunting knife and show the dumb twit what a real blade was all about.

An hour before that Law had contemplated blowing the head of a clown inside of the Big Top complex. He had no doubt that beneath the garish white paint and red wig lie an insatiable pedophile just waiting for a distracted parent to let go of the hand of a prepubescent child long enough for him to whip little bozo out of his ridiculous clown pants.

And 45 minutes before that he'd stood on the 3rd hole of a dinosaur-themed miniature golf course and weighed the odds of getting away with stuffing his putter down the throat of a balding tourist from Toledo. The man had made the mistake of telling his 9 year-old son, loud enough for Law to hear a hole away, that they turned the Falls off each night using a big wheel valve.

But Law had resisted all of those urges because today he was on a scouting mission only. The time for action would come soon, but before he could send another message to Mick O'Malley and the world he needed to find just the right venue for the job.

As he turned away from the shrunken head, Law decided that this was the place. He was standing inside of the Crowley's Believe It Or Don't Museum. Or rather, one of 55 such museums scattered around the globe.

The fact that the abominations were so numerous in number was one compelling reason to send his next message from this spot. It bothered Law on general principle that anyone would think there existed a need to divert attention away from the most splendid waterfalls in the world. The fact that it was accomplished with a franchise chain featuring all sorts of abnormalities and oddities just served to incense him even more.

Jonathan Richard Crowley thought Law, *what a waste of carbon molecules. A failed actor, he instead spent his life digging up every two-headed pickled punk he could find before slapping them on display to be ogled by every bohunk who had an extra two bits jingling around in his pocket.*

Law stepped outside and lit a cigarette as the twilight sky above him turned a brilliant shade of pink. A mother and teenaged daughter stood adjacent to the madman masquerading behind a kindly smile and debated aloud whether the $18.99 admission fee was worth it or not.

"You've got to go inside. It's a must see for sure," Law offered as he tapped his smoke out and placed the butt in a nearby trashcan.

"Really," said the teen, her pretty pug nose turning up as her brown eyes starred hard at Law. "It's looks kinda cheesy."

"Au contraire, my dear. It's the greatest thing since Bluetooth technology. You'll kick yourself if you don't go in."

The two women looked at each other, shrugged their shoulders and fished out a Visa card to purchase tickets. Law smiled at them as they hurried through the turnstile then said to no one in particular, "Believe it or don't."

CHAPTER 10

The day the Law manifesto hit the streets on the pages of the *Insider* is one that I will remember for the rest of my life. I awoke to a ringing telephone and answered to find a reporter from the *Washington Post* on the other end of the line. Over the next four hours I conducted interviews with such national media power-houses as *USA Today, the Chicago Tribune, the Boston Herald, the New York Times, Time and Newsweek.*

After a quick lunch ordered in, I went on to round two with a spate of local and national radio interviews. The questions ranged from the expected, "Why do you think Law is doing this?" and "Who is the man behind the madness?" to the ridiculous, "If Law were a tree, what tree would he be?"

As I was doing my best to placate the nation's newfound interest in the psycho-killer du jour, Johnny Guts was doing a great job of acting as my press agent by fielding interview requests at the *Insider* offices and patching them through to me at my home.

It was just after 5 PM when the phone rang and Johnny was on the other end with two pieces of information that would tear me in different directions.

"Hey Mick, how you holding up?"

"Pretty good Johnny, other than the fact that I'm losing my voice."

"Yeah, well I haven't exactly been resting the old windpipe myself over here. But listen Mick, I'm calling 'bout a couple of things. First, all of the network morning shows want you on tomorrow and ABC called and they want you to fly to L.A. and do the Jimmy Kimmel Show."

"Holy Shit, Johnny. This is really crazy. I mean pinch me, right? Tell ABC no, I'm not flying to California. But New York City is a different matter altogether. See if the *Today Show* will agree to let me be interviewed by Savannah Guthrie. She's really hot a…"

Before I could get another syllable out Johnny cut me off.

"Listen before I start booking your national tour there's something else you have to know. (Lowering his voice) There's a dame out in the waiting room asking to speak to you. She's got a shiner over her left eye. When I asked her who gave it to her, she said, 'Law.'"

"Don't let her go anywhere, Johnny. I'll be there in 10 minutes."

"Don't worry Mick, she's not going anywhere. We're both locked in. The local TV stations have been banging on the door for hours. When you get here come up the back stairs, the full media circus is camped out front."

CHAPTER 11

June 7th

I hopped into my Honda Accord Sport and raced over to the offices of the *Insider*. Along the way I called Sally and asked her to meet me there. I pulled around back and shut my engine off and waited for Sal to arrive. There were at least four news towers out front, but I was pretty sure I had avoided detection.

Ten minutes later, Sal's police issued black Chevy Impala pulled in next to me. She jumped out and slid into my front seat.

"Thanks for calling, Mick. She might be freaked out to see a cop with you so let me explain to her up front why I'm here. I've handled dozens of assault cases and I know how jittery women who have been abused can get."

"I'm a little jittery myself, Sal, but let's get up there before she flies the coop on us."

As we approached the back door of the office building I was nearly driven to a heart attack when someone jumped out at us from behind the paper recycling dumpster.

"Any truth to the rumor that there's a Law victim in your offices, Mick? How about you Detective, care to comment?" asked the man that I quickly recognized as *Morning News* Homicide Beat Writer Jeffery Lordes.

I was just about to tell Lordes just what I thought of him, his parentage and his flimsy excuse for a newspaper when I was beat to the punch by a very angry Sally Wendt.

"Lordes, I'm off-duty and if I have to come on-duty to deal with a roly-poly lowlife hack who likes to jerk off behind paper recyclers, I'm going to be the bitch from hell you wish you'd never crossed today. Am I making myself clear or do I need to clock in and show you my angry side?"

"Listen, I don't want to upset you Det…"

Sally cut him off with a glare that could curdle fresh milk.

"Why are you still here, little man?"

"Ah, I'm not here. I'm leaving. Good-bye," Lordes said as his pudgy little legs carried him off in cartoon-like fashion.

We entered the office to find Johnny Guts sitting alone on a couch in the lobby.

"Where's the woman?" I asked.

"She's in your office, Mick. Said she needed a couple of minutes alone. Mick, it's Melanie, Melanie Reese."

"Assistant District Attorney Dan Reese's wife?" Sal asked the question that I was thinking. I knew Dan and Melanie well as Dan had written quite a few columns for the *Insider* back when he was putting himself through law school.

"One and the same. I hate to break this to you, Sal, but he's the one that cold-cocked her."

Sal and I exchanged a look that said that we both realized that we'd gone from the frying pan straight into the burning gates of hell. If upright, family man, deacon of his church, pillar of the community Dan Reese was Law the city of Niagara Falls was fucked for all time. It would be a PR disaster that would sully the city's reputation for maybe all of the 12,000 years that scientists say the waterfalls have left.

I swallowed hard and turned the handle to my office.

Melanie Reese sat behind my desk with her head in her hands. The statuesque 28 year-old brunette was attractive in the way that women coming from old money always seem to be. She had an Eastern European air about her. Her face was comprised of long fluid lines that would have appealed to any number of Renaissance artists. Her folded hands featured long nimble fingers with nails finely polished with a French manicure. Everything about her spoke the words "strength" and "class," except for the growing mouse under her left eye.

"Hi, Melanie," I said as she looked up, happy to hear my voice, but showed alarm at Sally's presence. "Mel, I think you know Sally Wendt. Sally's handling the Law investigation and I thought she should be here to hear what you have to say."

"I didn't want the police involved. Not yet anyway. I was hoping that you could help me talk Dan into turning himself in, Mick. I didn't know who else to turn to." Melanie managed to get out before bursting into tears.

Sal went over and put an arm on her shoulder.

"I'm going to have a doctor take a look at it, but Mrs. Reese can you tell us what happened to your eye?"

"I confronted Dan about my suspicions. I told him that I thought he was Law. He'd been drinking all afternoon – sidecars. He told me I was crazy, said I was reading Mick's rag too much. When I told him I was going to turn him in he hit me and then drove off on his motorcycle."

"When did this happen?" Sal asked.

"A couple of hours ago."

Sal looked at her watch.

"It's 6:02 now, so around 4 o'clock then?

Melanie Reese nodded.

"Why do you think Dan is Law, Mel? It doesn't seem possible," I asked as I handed her a tissue for her tears.

"He's been distant for months now. No attentiveness, no sex. He's become obsessed with putting criminals away. He lost a big murder case last month and told me that he felt like taking out the son of a bitch himself. He always says 'The law has a name and it's spelled D-A-N.'"

"Still, that doesn't make him out to be a mass murderer, Mrs. Reese," Sally offered.

"No, but this does," Melanie Reese said as she opened her purse and handed me a sheet of paper, "I found this in his files."

"It's a letter from Dan to Lauren Tate dated May 15th," I explained to Sally.

"Go ahead, you can read it out loud," Melanie said.

"It says, 'Dear Miss Tate, Pursuant to our last conversation please be advised that you are in violation of the representation agreement we set forth in a contract dated April 23rd of this year. From a legal perspective let there be no misunderstanding of the fact that I will sue you for every penny you've got if you don't honor our agreement in full. On a personal note, don't even let yourself dream that I won't hurt you permanently if you screw me over. Yours Truly, Dan Reese.'"

"Do you have any idea what agreement he was referring to, Mrs. Reese?" Sally queried.

"No. All he told me was that she was the cash cow that he was going to retire on."

CHAPTER 12

Sally called for an ambulance for Melanie Reese and insisted that the responding EMTs take her over to Memorial Medical Center to have her eye checked out more closely. Once the protesting wife of the assistant DA turned mass murderer suspect was taken away Sal, Johnny and I flopped onto the Insider's lobby couches and tried to make some sense of the freight train that had just run us over.

"There's no way it can be Reese, is there?" asked Johnny.

"Well, right now there is at least cause to bring him in for questioning," answered Sal as she phoned in to have an APB put out to do just that.

"I've known Dan Reese since he was a green-behind-the-ears college freshman. When he wrote for me here he used to carry spiders outside to set them free. I just can't make him for Law," I offered.

"Well, unless you've got any other leads he's the only suspect we have at the moment." Sal said. "Let's recap what we know, or think we know. First, Law uses plastic explosives to blow up a helicopter and kill Lauren Tate."

"Any reason to believe that Reese knew anything about explosives?" Johnny asked.

"He's in the reserves. Did an extended tour in Afghanistan with the 914th Airlift Wing, just got back in February. He might have worked with plastic explosives there," I said.

Sal was taking notes as fast as her hand could write.

"I'll get ahold of his CO and see if Uncle Sam had Danny boy blowing things up on the taxpayer nickel. Let's examine the AquaticWorld killings. Is it possible Law is Canadian?"

"Sure it's possible, but it ain't probable," Johnny answered. "I been in this city my whole life. On the whole we're a lot more barbaric in the good old U.S of A. than they are over on the 'C' side. My money says Law is as American as bringing a lawsuit."

"My gut says you're right Johnny, though I can't attribute it to such jingoistic roots. I do believe that people tend to be passionate about their local paper. The fact that Law picked Mick as his sounding board probably means that he lives right here in Niagara Falls, New York," Sal stated just as she got a call on her cell phone.

"Yeah, it's Wendt. Whadaya got? Shit. I'll be right there."

"Sal, what is it?" I asked.

"It's Reese. A black and white pulled him over on his motorcycle out on River Road. When the officer tried to get him into the patrol car Reese pulled out a handgun and began firing. The officer only suffered a flesh wound, but Reese escaped and is on the run again."

"What the fuck has gone wrong around here?" Johnny Guts mouthed the question that we were all asking ourselves.

CHAPTER 13

Have you ever noticed how life sometimes has a way of really fucking with you? You know, throwing you a curve ball when you're still trying to catch up with the heater that has been blowing by you all night?

The morning after the Reese cop shooting I woke and found a text on my phone from Lisa Wilson asking me to give her a call. Lisa runs an anti-bullying teen peer group that meets once a week at the LaSalle Library. The kids have all been bullied and many of them have reacted to their horrific upbringings by cutting themselves or even attempting suicide.

I got her on the phone and Lisa said that their guest speaker had bailed on them last minute and wanted to know if I could fill in? I would have rather signed up to slam my hand in a car door repeatedly, but heard my mouth uttering the words, "Uh, sure, 7 pm, right?" before I hung up the phone and wondered what in the hell I would talk about.

There was no new news on the Reese manhunt throughout the day. Johnny was in Buffalo Court because his alcoholic, gambling addicted, work-avoiding ex-wife decided she needed more alimony, most likely to cover her expanding thirst and dwindling luck with the slot machines. Sal was hunkered down with Carlson and the rest of the FBI plotting their next move if Reese was cleared as not being the madman known as Law.

So I spent the afternoon paying some bills and working out what I would talk to the teens about. I finally decided that I would center my talk on writing and the therapeutic effects of creating poetry or keeping a journal to deal with emotional issues before they led one to the dark side.

That night I met Lisa at the main doors to the Library and she led me up to the 2nd floor meeting room. I stepped inside and was greeted with the expectant stares of fifteen teenagers. A few of them seemed to be excited to see someone other than Lisa show up to speak to them. Most however, had that "what could this douche possibly have to say that would even remotely interest me" look that teens have perfected since the very first societies formed thousands of years ago.

Well, at least they're not staring at their Smart phones, I thought before plowing ahead with my barely sketched-out presentation.

To my surprise I sailed along better than I thought I would and the hour that had been allotted for me flew by pretty quickly. I found that the kids became quickly engaged and I even followed-up my speech with a Q&A session that drew a lot of queries.

There was a refreshment period that followed. As the kids wolfed down some Sammy's Pizza and chugged some Johnnie Ryan Birch Beer I was making small talk with Lisa as some of their parents began showing up to cart them back home.

A mom in her early 30s with jet black hair, deep brown eyes and a facial structure that hinted at a heritage that found roots in the Caribbean came to collect a girl by the name of Ayesha. Spotting me, she stopped in her tracks and motioned for her daughter to retake her seat.

"Aren't you the man from the newspaper?" she asked in an accent that might have greeted a first-time visitor to the beaches of Jamacia.

"Mick O'Malley," I said as I nodded my head and extended my hand.

"Manuela Morgan. You might not remember, but we had an economics class together in college. Professor Mansfield, if I recall correctly."

"Oh yeah, 'Marble Mouth' Mansfield. How could I ever forget? How is life treating you Manuela?"

"Well, that's what I was hoping to talk to you about, Mick. Is it okay that I call you Mick?"

"Sure," I answered.

"Great. Listen, Mick," she continued as she lowered her voice by more than a few decibels. "My ex, Darnell, is a cop on the force. He gets Ayesha on the weekends. Lately she's been coming home with marks on her body. They look like belt marks, like she's been beaten. When I ask her if her daddy is hurting her, she won't answer. She just shuts me out."

"Does he have a history of abuse?" I ask.

Manuela nods slowly as if the pain of the memory she's experiencing is inflicting her anew.

"He used to drink heavily when we were married. Said the pressures of the job required him to let off steam by taking a shot or two. Jack Daniels was his drink of choice. He was a nasty drunk. First couple of drinks he'd be laughing. Two or three more and it usually ended with him trying to smash my head through the wall. I reported him to the Office of Professional Standards and was told to 'let the department handle it from within.' One night, when Ayesha was 7 he nearly drowned me in the bathtub while yelling that he was coming for her next. I packed up a U-Haul and moved back in with my mother the next day. Our divorce became final 9 months later."

"I'm sorry to hear all of that, but what can I do for you?"

"Ayesha come here," Manuela intoned.

When the girl complied, her mother lifted up the back of her shirt to reveal a half dozen bruises and welts that made me wince despite my attempts to refrain.

"He's going to truly hurt this child, maybe kill her. He's back on the drink and he is taking his frustrations with the world out on her. I'd call the police, but, honestly, Darnell's alimony and child support payments are the only thing keeping our heads above water right now. Please Mick, I know your newspaper gives you influence. Help me stop him before it's too late for my baby girl."

Despite my inclination to the contrary I heard myself saying, "Sure, no worries."

CHAPTER 14

June 13th

Jack Finch slipped his key into the lock and turned the dead bolt to secure the front door of the Bubble Jet Tours of Niagara. Finch had opened the successful sightseeing business in Niagara-on-the-Lake, a beautiful Victorian town 15 miles north of the Falls, a dozen years ago.

The Bubble Jets were a collection of high-power boats designed to navigate the dangerous Class 5 rapids that ran North of the Whirlpool in the lower Niagara River.

The boats were constructed to take up to 50 passengers at a time on a high-speed thrill ride that made the boats that got up close to the falls seem tame by comparison. The highlight of the Bubble Jet experience was what was known as the Hamilton turn. It was when the boat's captain took it full-speed into the mighty Whirlpool and made it hydroplane on it's side diagonally, cutting a path directly through the center of the giant swirling eddy.

When Finch first proposed the attraction there was a lot of resistance from people that felt that the noise of the boats' engines would destroy the serenity found on the hiking trails at the bottom of the gorge.

Still others believed that the wakes created by the thrust of the engines would cause irrevocable damage to the shoreline. There was much clamoring at the open meetings that were held for public input.

Finch spoke eloquently in favor of the economic impact that his boats would bring and lined enough pockets on both sides of the border to make a master seamstress green with envy.

The Bubble Jets quickly became a "must do" attraction and Jack Finch rapidly became rich. His swanky office had two picture windows. One looked out on his operations on the lower river. The other offered an unobstructed view of the parking lot and the jet black Lamborghini parked in the spot with his name on it that was his pride and joy.

Finch used the auto-start button on his key fob to get the big 8-cylinder engine purring on his midlife crisis car. He then pushed the button to pop the trunk so that he could toss in the bank bag he was carrying with the day's impressive receipts.

Just then a figure moved quickly out of the shadows and a gloved hand holding a rag soaked in chloroform was pressed unyieldingly into the mouth and nose of Jack Finch. The boat entrepreneur fought gamely, but soon his world went black and he hit the ground with a sickening thud.

"Wakey, Wakey hands off snakey," said the madman known as Law as Jack Finch slowly began to regain consciousness.

"Where am I, what's happened, who the fuck are you?" Finch asked as the reality of his terrible circumstances began to take focus.

Finch was naked and he was both hand and ankle shackled tightly to a long table that would not have been out of place at a morgue. His vision was still blurry, but he began to notice that he was surrounded by a bevy of what appeared to be human heads and assorted body parts.

"One question at a time my huckleberry," said Law as he placed an icepick on the table next to Finch.

"Where you are is in the preparation and repair room of the

Crowley's Museum. What has happened is that you have been a very naughty boy with your river-destroying boats. As to who I am, let's just say I am the angel of retribution and I'm going to help transition you to the fiery pits that are your eternal destiny."

"Look if you want money, just name the amount. I can make a call and…"

Finch's sentence was cut short by a vicious blow to the jaw from Law that drew a torrent of gushing blood.

"Quiet, you insolent fool. Do I look like a common criminal in search of an easy buck? I wouldn't accept a dime of your accursed money if I was starving to death in the streets."

Finch tried to say something, but the pool of blood in his mouth made his words come out as one long unintelligible garble.

"Shhh, save your breath, it won't do you any good anyway. You, my doomed friend, are on trial and I will serve on behalf of the prosecution and will also offer up your sentencing should you be deemed guilty."

Law reached down and lifted up a vat filled with molten wax.

"It's truly creepy how they make these monstrosities of celebrities that take up residence in this ungodly place. Creepy, but efficient. Mr. Jack Finch you are hereby charged with crimes against nature for the damage to the Niagara River caused by your fleet of boats. How do you plead?"

Finch again tried to speak, but the blood and the aching in his broken jaw prevented him for properly forming any words found in a standard dictionary.

"I'll take that as 'Not Guilty,'" said Law as he stirred the glowing hot wax with a wooden ladle.

"Mr. Finch, the prosecution believes this to be an open and

shut case. We believe that the judge, namely me, will easily see that your nefarious deeds in the pursuit of the almighty dollar have indelibly scarred one of the most beautiful rivers in all the world and that your punishment must be both swift and severe."

Finch began to struggle mightily against his shackles all to no avail.

"Your boats, Mr. Finch, have polluted the waters of the lower Niagara with their emissions and have polluted the surrounding air with noise that has spoiled what once was one of the most serene hikes in all the universe. The erosive damage to the shoreline is as sinister as it is malicious. You have known of the carnage that your operation causes for years and you have used your deep pockets to buy off many in power so that your evil enterprise could continue on unimpeded while you fattened your bank account all the while. Now, have you anything to offer in your own defense?"

Finch tried again to speak but could offer no decipherable words.

"Not surprising," Law concluded. "The guilty have no alibi. In that instance I rest my case and I simultaneously sentence you to death by wax."

As Law concluded, Finch again began straining hard against the ties that secured his four limbs.

"Now, I am not a man without a heart, Mr. Finch. I will offer you one last come before you go," Law stated as he flipped on a computer screen that was mounted on the wall above Finch.

The screen was immediately filled with the image of a naked young woman with her legs spread open wide.

"Let's see are cheerleaders your thing?" Law asked.

"No? How about gangbangs?" then clicking to a new video,

"Does that, pardon the pun, float your boat?"

On the screen a nubile Asian woman was on her hands and knees sucking on one giant member while another slammed in and out of her from behind.

"No response to that one either. Ah, I know what you like, lesbians."

Law once again clicked and suddenly two blonde girls were seen locked in a 69 position as they simultaneously licked and moaned their way to pure ecstasy. Despite his dire circumstances, Jack Finch felt his penis engorging with blood.

"So typical," said Law as he saw Finch rising to a full erection.

Finch couldn't look away as the girls on the screen were gyrating and grinding their wet kitties into each other's mouths. His mind tried to think of something, anything else, but his throbbing manhood would have none of it. Good God no, he thought, don't let it happen. But, to his horror, he felt his balls tighten. Jack Finch let out a muffled moan and a huge rope of ejaculate shot from his throbbing penis. In one swift move Law grabbed the vat of molten wax and brought it down on the startled Finch covering his still erect member as the boatman's moan turned to a blood-curdling scream.

Before Finch could fully comprehend what was happening to him, Law picked up the ice pick and jammed it into his temple. Death, in this case, was indeed merciful as the plans that Law had for the corpse were ones that no man would wish to be alive to experience.

"They're going to be in for quite a shock tomorrow, even for this freak show of a street," said Law as he reached under the table and retrieved a machete.

CHAPTER 15

It was early afternoon and I'd already felt like I'd put in a full weeks worth of hours. I'd called Sal and inquired about Darnell Morgan. I'd found out that he'd had a few recent disciplinary marks on his record for getting rough with suspects he'd arrested.

The most recent was a street-level weed seller that he'd pistol-whipped into confessing to a corner store robbery. Problem was the pot pusher was black and two witnesses gave statements that the guy that jacked the 7-11 was white as the pure-driven snow.

I told Sal about my discussion with Manuela and the marks I saw on the body of young Ayesha.

"That son-of-a-bitch, I knew he was nothing but a pile of stinking garbage," Sal said through clenched teeth.

"What can we do?" I asked. "Manuela is sure that his shield will protect him from any disciplinary action."

"She's right, the old guard will circle around him, but not all cops observe the blue wall of silence. We've got 15 female officers on the force and there is nothing that we hate more than a dickless cretin posing as an officer who takes his shortcomings out on a defenseless child. Let me give Melissa Dunton a call. She's a social worker with County and she's great at working the system to protect kids in danger."

"Thanks, Sal. I would feel awful if something worse happened to that kid."

I'd also received word that Dan Reese was still on the loose, but that his motorcycle had been spotted near Grundy Provincial Park in Britt, ON.. Evidently, he had a summer cabin out that way and the OPP had it staked out and were hopeful that he would turn up and they could take him into custody.

I hadn't seen Johnny Guts in nearly 48 hours and was getting worried. Just then the phone rang and I snatched it the way that an Olympic runner might grab a baton.

"Mick, it's Johnny. I just got word from one of my Niagara Regional Police sources in Ontario that Jack Finch, you know the Bubble Jet guy, was found murdered this morning. So far, the *Morning News* hasn't gotten a whiff of it, but it won't be long before Lordes gets tipped off. You'd better head over there."

In minutes flat, I was at Customs and then at the Niagara Regional Police Office. I asked for Constable Doyle an old friend.

"Mick, you old dog, How are you?"

"I'm good Ronnie. How are Cathy and the kids?"

'They're all great. Brian, my oldest, started University this year. He's going to Brock on a full-ride, hockey scholarship. Takes after the old man."

"That's great. I'll have to come over and catch a game with you," I responded.

"Sure thing. What brings you over to my side of the river, Mick?"

"I understand Jack Finch was found murdered, what can you tell me?"

"How in the hell did you hear that? The upper echelon has that hammered down shut. We've all been ordered not to breathe a word of it until they hold the press conference this afternoon. We were told it was immediate termination if it was our lips that were loose."

"You know me, Ronnie. Some guys whisper to horses, birds always seem to sing in my ear."

Constable Doyle looked both ways and grabbed me by the elbow and walked me outside and away from the police building.

"Look Mick, you know you're like a brother to me. Even though we both bleed the green of ol' Ireland, I can't tell you much. As I said it's on heavier lockdown than anything I've ever seen in my twenty years on the force. What I can tell you is that his body was found in the window of the Crowley's Museum on Clifton Hill and that Jack Finch had been violated in ways that a man of decency should never have to experience."

"Christ, Ronnie. Do you think there is a connection to Law?" I asked.

"We're sure of it Mick," Doyle answered.

"Why's that?"

"Because there was a message written to you in Finch's blood at the scene."

CHAPTER 16

I'd barely left Ronnie and made it over the Rainbow Bridge and through customs back into the US when my cell phone rang and Sally Wendt's name popped up on my dashboard hands-free screen.

"Hey, Sal. What's up?"

"Jack Finch, you know the owner of the Bubble Jets, has turned up as Law's latest victim. His body was found in the display window of Crowley's Believe It or Don't on Clifton Hill."

"Wow, that's crazy," I responded, deciding to protect both Johnny Guts' and Ronnie Doyle's info from Sally for now.

"Yeah, what's more is I've been told that the crime scene is as grisly as they come and that there is a message to you written out in the blood of Jack Finch."

"Damn," I said with conviction that I hoped would mask the fact that Sally's bombshell was old news to my ears.

"Where are you? We need to be at Niagara Regional Police Headquarters at 4 PM. They are going to brief us on the details and show video of the crime scene before we hold a joint press conference today at 6 PM."

"I'm just heading back to my office," I offered, while wondering how many times one can cross the Canadian border in one day without arousing the suspicions of a customs agent.

"Great, I'll pick you up at 3:30 and we can ride over together. Carlson will make a statement for the American investigation, but you and I will be expected to field questions from the press."

Sally hung up and I made the turn on First Street headed to Buffalo Avenue. *Fuck,* I thought to myself, *we're all just marionettes and Law is the lunatic pulling our strings.*

"Why Jack Finch?" I asked Sally after we'd cleared customs and made the left hand turn onto River Road heading toward Niagara Regional Police Headquarters.

"Hard to figure. His boats brought a lot of money and jobs to both sides of the border. He seemed to be universally admired and gave tens of thousands of dollars to local charities every year," Sal responded, "Maybe Law made it clear at the crime scene."

Moments later we pulled into Police HQs and were greeted at the door by Ronnie Doyle.

"Hi Mick, this is Captain Richard Sutcliffe, he's heading up the Law investigation for our agency," Ronnie deadpanned with a poker face that would please the ghost of John Scarne.

"Hello Captain Sutcliffe, this is Detective Sally Wendt of the Niagara Falls Police Force," I said.

"We've had the pleasure before. Good to see you again, Sally, though the circumstances are a bit lacking," said Capt. Sutcliffe.

"Good to see you, too, Dick. What can you tell us about the Finch murder?"

"It's the most barbaric I've ever seen, Sally," Sutcliffe responded as he ushered her and I into a briefing room outfitted with a table and six chairs along with a laptop connected to a flatscreen TV, "Can I get you a coffee or water?"

"I'll take a cup of tea if you have one," Sally responded.

"Tea, eh? You do have a bit of Canadian in you now, Sally. And you, Mick?"

"I'll have a Coke please."

Sutcliffe motioned for Ronnie to fetch the drinks and settled into his chair while opening up a file folder teeming with papers on the Finch killing.

"Jack Finch was last heard from by anyone that knew him yesterday evening at 9 PM when the last employee left the Bubble Jet offices after they closed for the day. Surveillance cameras show a shrouded man coming up behind Finch at precisely 9:27 PM and forcing a rag – we now know that it was doused with chloroform – over his mouth. The man then stuffs Finch into the trunk of the car. We see the car head south on Queen Street before the camera loses it. We spot the car intermittently on various cameras as it heads south on the Niagara Parkway. Eventually, it turns west onto Bridge Street and we lose it for good as it turns south again into a residential neighborhood. Of course we now know that he ended up breaking into Crowley's Museum sometime after they closed at 1 AM," Sutcliffe explained.

A knock was heard at the door and Ronnie answered it and let in Agent Carlson, who took a seat next to Sally.

"Why Crowley's?" I asked.

"I think that will be abundantly clear once you see the crime scene, Mr. O'Malley. Welcome Agent Carlson. I've briefed them on the events of last night from the file that we shared with your office earlier today. Ronnie, roll the footage, will you? I caution you all that, even by the standards associated with our line of work, what you are about to witness is truly inhumane and evil."

Ronnie Doyle clicked a few keys on the laptop and hit the light switch to darken the room. The TV screen flickered to life and was immediately filled with an image that will haunt me to my last breath.

"As you can see," Capt. Sutcliffe spoke in a slow, deliberate drawl, "Mr. Finch was found in this position in the front window of the Crowley's lobby."

It was beyond horrific. A fully-naked Jack Finch was propped up over a sawhorse, on all fours. There was a pool of blood on the floor in the area just beneath his legs. An ice pick was still lodged in the side of his head. The tip of something was protruding from his anus as was something showing just beyond the lips of his mouth.

"We are still awaiting the full autopsy report but believe Mr. Finch's time of death to be between 2 and 3:30 AM. The cause of death appears to be trauma resulting from an ice pick plunged into Mr. Finch's left temple. Mercifully, that happened before his penis was severed with a sharp knife," Sutcliffe said, his voice now breaking as he conveyed the manner of death of one of his city's finest citizens.

Carlson remained stoic as I thought I saw the hint of tears forming in Sally's eyes. As for me, for the first time in my life, I truly thought I was going to faint.

The camera circled around the body in slow, agonizing arcs. It would occasionally stop in one area and zoom in for a closer examination of something that I wouldn't have wanted to view from Pluto using the Hubble Telescope.

"You'll notice that Mr. Finch has been violated both orally and anally," Capt. Sutcliffe continued as his voice cracked once again, "In both instances by wax phalluses formed from his own erect penis."

"Jesus," I said aloud.

"Fuck," added a no-longer stoic Agent Carlson.

"What you will see next is of most interest to Mr. O'Malley. I warn you again, it's as demonic as I've ever witnessed."

Written on the display window in bold, block letters of dripping Jack Finch blood was a message leaving no ambiguity about Law's future intentions.

Finch is just the canary in the coal mine. Silent death is coming to all that don't respect the beauty of the Falls. Tell them Mick - they can run, but they can't hide from the Law.

I felt all the blood run from my head and I grabbed the edges of the table to keep from going down.

Sally put her hand on mine and whispered to me to breathe in through my nose and out through my mouth.

"That, folks, is what we know. There were no fingerprints found at the scene. There was some fiber evidence collected, but with the high traffic that Crowley's sees we have no way to conclusively connect it to Law. We still have an APB out for Dan Reese, as we, like the FBI, consider him our number one suspect, but we have not ruled out anyone as a suspect at this time," Sutcliffe concluded as Ronnie Doyle clicked off the video.

"Captain Sutcliffe, on behalf of the FBI I thank you for the briefing. I am calling for more manpower as we must apprehend Law before anyone else is murdered. I'll see you shortly for the press conference," Agent Carlson said as he stood and extended his hand to Sutcliffe.

Sally and I stood up and did likewise. My legs still felt like rubber beneath me.

"What do you plan on writing in the paper, Mick?" Carlson asked.

"Exactly what he asked me to," I offered and stepped outside for a much-needed breath of fresh air.

CHAPTER 17

The press conference went according to script and, once again, two countries were consumed with a new murder committed by a familiar perpetrator. I went back to my apartment and wanted nothing more than to turn off my brain and somehow erase the images of the defiled Jack Finch from my memory bank forever.

I popped two Tylenol PMs and swallowed two melatonins as a chaser. Soon I fell into a deep, albeit disturbed, slumber. The combination of pills caused me to have a series of twisted, lurid dreams. In one I was drowning in a pool of ever-deepening blood. In another, Sara had turned the tables on me and I was the one shackled to the bed, naked on all fours, while she crouched behind me with a giant dildo and said, "Prepare to be Finched, Mick."

Thankfully, I was rescued from my subconscious trip through the deepest levels of hell by a pounding on my door.

"Mick, it's Sally. Open up if you're in there," I heard as I struggled to get my arms into my bathrobe.

"Oh, Hi, Sal," I said as I opened the door.

"Hi, Sal? For chrissakes Mick, it's nearly noon. I've been calling and texting you for hours."

"Sorry, I self-medicated last night to get to sleep after watching that crime scene video and I guess I popped one too many pills."

"Look, I know seeing something like that isn't easy, but suck it up buttercup, I don't need you checking out of Hotel Mick early on me. We've got a bad guy to catch, remember?"

"Sure. Any news?" I asked while stumbling around the kitchen trying to get the coffee maker started.

"Not on Law, but I do have the skinny on Darnell Morgan. I did some digging around and found out that aside from the incidences I told you about Internal Affairs investigated him three years ago for abusing a side chick by the name of (checking her notes) Felicia Bradley. He beat her pretty badly, including leaving large welts on her body that matched, in size and design, a brass belt buckle found at his residence."

"That son-of-a-bitch," I exclaimed.

"Don't blame it on his mother, Mick. Morgan more than likely got his misogynistic tendencies from his paternal heritage. I.A. was ready to file charges and put him on suspension when Ms. Bradley informed them she would no longer cooperate and announced her intentions to move to Florida to live with her half-sister."

"Morgan got to her, threatened her somehow," I said as I felt anger boiling in my veins.

"That's my guess, but there's more. I also found out that there is a current investigation and that Morgan is suspected of being the ringleader of a small group of rogue, dirty cops. They have reputedly stolen money, drugs and jewelry from crime scenes and have a network of contacts to fence the goods and resell the drugs on the street. My Captain has a hard-on for Morgan and wants all the ducks in order so that when they take him down it will stick like superglue on taffy."

"Then the bastard did abuse Ayesha," I said.

"It certainly appears that way. Mick."

"Goddamn it. My head is all screwed up because of Law, but

we've got to help that little girl, Sal."

"I know, Mick. I did get to speak with Melissa Dunton. She made a visit out to see Ayesha and has put her under the watch of Child Protective Services. I also called Darnell into my office this morning. I told him that Ayesha and Manuela were under my protection."

"You did? Holy shit, what did he say? I asked.

"He started to get mouthy and tried to intimidate me they way that he does the other females in his life. I told him that he knew a lot of bitches, but he was now dealing with the Queen Bitch. He said, 'You trying to stab me in the back?'"

"What did you say?" I asked.

"I said, 'Don't worry your pretty little head, Darnell. When I take you down I'll be coming straight at you.'"

CHAPTER 18

June 22nd

It was a sunny late morning in the third week of June and Dan Reese was in the back of a tour bus at customs on the United States side of the Rainbow Bridge. He could feel his heart beating through his chest as he silently reminded himself to control his breathing. Reese had purchased the tour from the lobby of the Fallsview Hilton in Niagara Falls, Ontario.

He had been staying at the luxury hotel under an assumed name for the past 8 days. The property, at 1,050 rooms the largest between New York City and Toronto, was one of his favorite hotels in all the world. It featured 4 restaurants – including The Watermark, which offered floor-to-ceiling panoramic views of all three Niagara Falls – along with two swimming pools, a spa, a nightclub featuring live music nightly, a 5,000 seat theater, direct connections to the Fallsview Casino and a staff well-versed in the fine art of customer service.

Reese had long ago learned that if you wanted a piece of information about what really went down at a hotel a bellman was your best bet. So he'd slipped a Benjamin into the hand of a tall, lanky bellman that wore a name tag denoting himself as "The Hook."

"If a guy wanted to cross the border with the least amount of governmental inspection how might he accomplish that?" Reese asked.

"Easy, go see the American at the tour desk," the Hook replied as he quickly tucked the C-note in his pants' pocket. "I thought you were going to ask for something difficult like uncut blow or a hooker with a reattached hymen."

So Dan Reese had slid in behind two couples from Albuquerque, New Mexico and feigned interest as the Hilton's Tourism Director laid out a honeyed pitch so smooth that Ron Popeil himself would have reached for his Ronco AMEX card to cement his place on the tour bus. Malcolm Gladwell famously said that a person needs a minimum of 10,000 hours at his craft before he can be considered an expert. *This guy has closer to 100,000 hours* thought Reese as the couples from the "Land of Enchantment" state gleefully signed up for the tour before he followed suit and did the same.

Reese desperately needed to get back into the United States to try and fix this mess that his life had become. How had things become so unraveled? How had all of his well-laid plans all gone awry? These thoughts haunted him both day and night and consumed every neuron in his brain. *It was that fucking Lauren Tate,* he thought, *that bitch screwed up everything.*

Reese knew that he would never be able to cross over the border on his motorcycle. Every agent was on high alert and he would surely be taken into custody before he was even able to declare his citizenship. As fate would have it, Reese had been at the Hilton's adults-only swimming pool when he noticed a man of his general age and build tuck his wallet into his sneaker for safe keeping as he went for a dip. Reese waited until he saw the man settle into the adjoining hot tub and close his eyes for a relaxing soak then the disgraced D.A. sprang into action.

He quickly went into the running shoe and got his hands on the wallet. Reese located and extracted the man's driver's license and gave an inner shout for joy when he saw that it had the prominent star symbol designating it as authorized for US/Canada border transit. He replaced the wallet without detection and exited the pool faster than a governmental employee leaving a federal building at the strike of 4 PM on a Friday afternoon.

When he got back to his room, Reese carefully memorized every piece of information on the license. Name, address, ID number and expiration date, which Reese knew was also the man's birthdate. The man was blonde, while Dan Reese had rich, black tresses of hair. That problem was solved by a quick trip to the closest drug store. *What was the old Miss Clairol commercial,* Reese thought, *Does she or doesn't she? Only her hairdresser knows for sure.*

And that's how dark-haired fugitive Dan Reese had become blonde Midwesterner Hank Goodrich from Sandusky, Ohio. Reese was gambling that a tour bus with 50 eager beavers all itching for their first ever close-up view of the world's most famous waterfalls would be his best bet to sneak through customs undetected. An agent had boarded the bus and was slowly walking the middle aisle after she'd asked all aboard to get their IDs out and hold them aloft. As Reese had hoped, her inspection of the passports, NEXUS cards and enhanced licenses was perfunctory. She was simply taking quick glances and checking to make sure that expiry dates were not in violation and that the people vaguely resembled the motley assortment of photos that littered the documents being held up.

Reese was in the second to last row. He had surmised that the further back in the bus the agent got the sloppier her inspections would become. She was just one row away now. In 15 seconds he was either going to raise her suspicions and be ultimately found out and removed from the bus handcuffed at the business end of a service revolver or he was going to be gleefully on his way, ostensibly to spend the afternoon taking in the sights and sounds of one of the world's great natural beauties.

Reese thought his heart was going to explode as the agent glanced at the stolen license before quickly
looking at his face. A second that seemed to last an eternity and boom it was over. The agent moved on to the last row and finished up before walking back to the front of the bus and announcing, "Great. Thanks, folks and welcome to the United States. Enjoy our waterfalls."

Reese stayed on the bus until it made a scheduled stop at the New York Power Vista. As the tour guide wrangled them off of the coach bus and began explaining how the falls generated enough hydroelectricity to light up 40% of the entire East Coast of the United States, Reese quietly stepped away from the group and used the burner phone he'd purchased in Canada to call a taxicab.

Reese gave the cab driver the address to an animal shelter in the small town of Model City, just a few miles from the Power Vista. Model City had been the brainchild of con man developer William T. Love. In the early 1890s, Love had come up with the idea to use the electricity generated by the Falls to create a utopian city of 2 million people just miles down river from the raging cataracts.

"Love sold a bill of goods to a lot of innocent people," A former local history curator at the Niagara Falls Library once said. "He dug a hole, then he left town."

It was estimated that Love raised millions of dollars from local governments eager to prosper from Niagara Falls and the money never re-emerged from his pockets – a practice still commonplace today.

Three events ultimately doomed Model City. First the depression of the 1890s dried up investments. Secondly, Nikola Tesla developed Alternating Current and it was no longer necessary for cities to be in close physical proximity to power sources as electricity could now be sent long distances away. Lastly, in 1907, Congress passed the Burton Act, which prohibited further diversion of the water from Niagara Falls.

Very little remained at Model City these days. Just a garbage dump, a post office and the animal shelter where Melanie Reese volunteered three days a week. Dan Reese waited ducked behind the rear bumper of the late model silver Mercedes-AMG CLS that his pampered wife had demanded for her 27th birthday.

Just then Melanie exited the shelter and the doors of the Mercedes unlocked as the advanced systems of the luxury car sensed her imminent arrival. Reese duck-walked around to the passenger side and as his wife entered the cabin he did likewise. She began to scream as she saw him, but he quickly put a hand over her mouth.

"It's okay, honey. Be cool. I'm not going to hurt you. Just do what I say. Okay? Can you do that?"

Melanie Reese nodded.

"Good girl. We're going on a little road trip. Get out to Route 104 and head east. The shit is about to hit the fan babydoll and we are not getting flushed down with it."

CHAPTER 19

Law put the tip of the unfiltered Camel in his mouth and pulled in hard. He closed his eyes as he felt the smoke hit his lungs and he held it there. He could feel the nicotine being carried into his bloodstream. The accompanying endorphins that his hypothalamus requested hit the opioid centers of his brain and the madman found himself in an R.J. Reynolds-induced state of bliss.

Blowing out the smoke into 5 expanding rings, Law surveyed the area around him. It was 2:00 AM on a moonless summer night. The only other living creatures out North of 103rd Street on the banks of Bergholtz Creek were the sandflies and mosquitos that were tormenting a man used to being the tormentor.

Dammit, I should have sprayed myself with some of that deep woods repellent, thought Law as he watched another hungry mosquito fly off with a few precious drops of his cold-as-ice blood.

Law was at the northernmost end of one of the most infamous sections of Niagara Falls – Love Canal.

When William T. Love's Model City dreams went belly up, the Panic of 1907 being the final nail in that coffin, he disappeared faster than a $50 bill into a crackhead whore's bra, but left behind an unfinished canal that was supposed to carry water from Niagara Falls to his utopian metropolis. That canal eventually filled with water and became a popular swimming spot for the children of the families living in the neighborhoods surrounding it.

8

The City of Niagara Falls in general, and Hooker Chemical in particular, spent decades dumping garbage and chemical waste into the waterway. In the 1970s those chemicals began surfacing as cancer rates soared in the families that lived on the old canal site. What's worse is that the city had built two grade schools on the site in the mid-1950s. Both the school board and Hooker Chemical knew of the tons of toxins that had been buried there, but didn't let that salient knowledge stand in the way of condemning the healthy futures of children that would one day become the future leaders of the Cataract City.

Love Canal became synonymous with environmental corruption as lawsuits led to national headlines that ultimately begat a massive cleanup effort at the site.

This is the epicenter of what happens when man's greed is allowed to take precedence over God's Plan, thought Law as he tapped out the last of his cigarette against a flat rock on the ground before slipping it into his pocket for proper disposal at a later time.

My plan is running smoothly, but the Lauren Tates and Jack Finches of the world are just one side of the equation of what's wrong at Niagara Falls. The other side, the one that has caused the most damage, are the chemical factories that have polluted the water of the Niagara River since the very first days of the industrial revolution. Hooker Chemical, of course, was the big whale that swam in those waters, but there were sharks like Union Carbide, Olin Chemical and Great Lakes Carbon that also used the Niagara River as their own personal pollutant playground.

Law looked around at the still mainly barren neighborhoods that surrounded him. He thought of the family pets that had died horrible deaths due to tumors and cancers too numerous to list. He thought of the elderly taking their last anguished breaths as the morphine pumped into their veins no longer brought comfort from the diseases that wrecked their bodies and crushed their souls. And he thought of the children, the innocents, doing nothing more natural than attending school and taking dips in a beloved swimming hole. Children, living their soon-to-be-cut-short lives amongst 21,800 tons of chemicals – 82 varieties that seeped up through the ground and poured into the basements of the homes that served as the foundation of their young lives. Lives that were sold by the stuffed suits that governed the school board and sat behind the management desks of a multitude of chemical corporations. And for what?

You don't need a mathematician to know that money is the root of all evil, thought the man who fancied himself an avenging angel. And for the first time since he'd stepped out of his car in Love Canal he spoke aloud.

"On this hallowed ground I will make a statement they can't ignore. One day we will have the embodiment of William T. Love's model city, one far greater and nobler than that charlatan could have ever imagined. Yes, we will have a Niagara Falls as God planned it, even if I have to kill every last motherfucker standing in the way to make it happen."

CHAPTER 20

June 25th

"Mick does my ass look huge in this dress?" Sara asked me as we were getting ready for Niagara Falls' Mayor Randolph Thompson's yearly ball.

"Are you kidding me, Sweetheart? Heads will be on a swivel all night to get a view of that sweet onion," I answered truthfully.

Sara made any outfit she put on look like it was created for her by a top fashion designer. Still there was something that always held her looks back from being truly elegant. She always ended up somewhere in that undefined zone of beauty found on the star meter between the words Hollywood and Porn.

"Now get those pretty little feet into some pumps because we are already 15 minutes behind schedule," I pleaded as I adjusted the cuff link on my left wrist.

French cuffs always befuddled me. There was almost no way to get the cuff links through the slots with the shirt on, yet my hands were too big to facilitate a proper execution if I put them in beforehand. I finally gave up and asked for help.

"Babe, can you get this for me?"

"Does my big, strong handsome man need help from his lady love? Seeing you in your tuxedo is getting me all wet, maybe you should rip off my panties and take me right here, Daddy," Sara said as she reached not for my sleeve, but for the zipper residing due South of it.

"Not now, Love. We have got to get going."

"Alright, buzz killer. But I expect a proper pounding when we get home tonight," Sara said as she adroitly locked in my cuff link.

Sara and I stepped into the ball and for a moment it felt like we were Tinseltown's hottest couple arriving on the red carpet. Sara was wearing a powder blue Stella McCartney knock-off dress with a plunging neckline. As we passed one table I overhead an old goat lean over to his friend and ask, "Don't they have a policy against bringing pets to these things?"

"Of course they do, why do you ask?" his friend replied.

"Then how did she get those puppies in here?" came the rejoinder as he motioned toward Sara's ample bosom and both old coots laughed like two hyenas at a fresh kill.

Sara was also wearing a set of white pearls that had belonged to my great-grandmother. They popped perfectly on her gown and made her blue eyes shine like the eternal water flowing over the Falls just a few miles away.

For my part, I had chosen a white tuxedo jacket with tails offset by a black bow tie and black slacks. On my feet were a natty pair of spectator shoes. I completed the ensemble by wearing my silver Bulova watch on one wrist and on the other a silver Gaelic bracelet featuring serpent heads at either end that I had purchased at a quaint little shop in Niagara-on-the-Lake.

The ball was being held at the swanky Seneca Niagara Casino Hotel. The 604-room, four diamond resort was attached to the casino of the same name. The casino had opened in 2003 and was thought by many to be the panacea so desperately needed by the Cataract City to drag it out of decades of declining population and fortune. Instead, it was more of a black hole in downtown Niagara Falls. It was a jewel and widely successful, but it had killed off almost all of the restaurants and other businesses that surrounded it. It was sort of like one tower in Emerald City surrounded by acres of the haunted forest.

As we made our way past the hors d'oeuvres trays and ice sculptures that adorned the white-cloth tables at the front of the room, we were waved over by the man-of-the-hour himself.

"Mick O'Malley, so glad you could make it. And who is this inhabitant of heaven you have on your arm my dear lad?" Mayor Thompson asked as his eyes made a quick dash up and down Sara's physique.

"This is my girlfriend, Sara Evans, Mayor. She works at Rumrunner Ray's," I responded.

"Of course, I knew I'd seen you before, my dear. A year ago last October when Niagara Rises held one of their 'Still Fallin' for the Falls' happy hours at your place, wasn't it?"

The mayor was referencing an upstart not-for-profit group of citizens that hoped to take the revival of Niagara Falls out of the politician's hands and into their own.

"Oh, yes sir. I do remember that," Sara replied as I marveled at the old scoundrel's ability to remember when and where he'd seen any pretty skirt over the past two decades.

"Listen Mick, I'll be giving a brief speech on the ugly Law nonsense a bit later in the evening. I do hope you'll cover it in the *Insider,* but if you do happen to cut out early please let the fair citizens of Niagara Falls know that I have instructed our police force to leave no stone unturned until we have this lunatic brought to justice and firmly behind bars. Can you do that for me, Mick?"

As he spoke I could almost hear a John Philip Sousa patriotic march playing in the air. Thompson was mostly a stuffed shirt, but he could spew out red, white and blue colored bullshit with the best of them.

"Sure thing, Mayor," I responded as, thankfully, one of the mayor's handlers whisked him away to press the flesh of a wealthy campaign contributor.

Sara and I made our way around the room sampling more than a couple of the flutes of complimentary champagne being passed out by white-gloved servers. We hit the dance floor and cut the rug to a few numbers being performed by the incomparable George Scott Orchestra. At that moment I was very thankful for the 8 weeks of lessons Sara had signed us up for that spring at the Arthur Murray Dance Studio.

Dinner was prepared courtesy of the students of the Niagara Culinary School. The appetizer was an Iceberg lettuce wedge salad with a creamy Italian dressing and bacon crumbles. The entrée was an exquisite Beef Wellington dish. The filet mignon center was cooked to just the right temperature so that it was teeming with flavor. The pâté and duxelles were made to perfection – the mushrooms, shallots, garlic, and thyme combining to create an intoxicating taste that danced the merengue on my tastebuds. The Parma ham and puff pastry outer shell completed the effect flawlessly. The sides were Dauphinoise potatoes and an asparagus with Hollandaise sauce. The praise for the dish was near universal and I felt a tinge of sorrow for the poor, misguided souls that had instead chosen the vegetarian option.

Dessert was the best crème brûlée I'd ever tasted in my life. The hardened caramelized sugar on the Trinity Cream was perfectly contrasted by the rich custard base. Sara had fun breaking through the top and I must admit that I got a little turned-on watching her pink tongue dart out to swallow the custard goodness from her spoon.

After dinner Sara excused herself to use the little girl's room and

I felt a hand touch me on the shoulder as a familiar voice drifted into my ear canal.

"Mick, my son, How are you enjoying the festivities?"

"Professor Brintkowski," I said as I motioned for him to take the seat next to me, "How nice it is to see you. How have you been?"

"Fair to middling, Mick. You know at my age aches and pains are par for the course, so long as I can get out and do the things that I love I don't complain too much."

"Speaking of things you love, Prof, how is the Greenway commission coming along?"

"Well, we're at a bit of a standstill while this Law character is creating havoc all over the city. Between you and me, Mick I hope they catch him before anyone else is murdered, but he's been good for business."

"What do you mean, Professor?"

"Well, no one agrees with his methods mind you, but his underlying message is one that we on the Greenway Commission have long espoused. Follow the Olmstead vision, first and foremost. Keep the falls natural and realize that they've been flowing for thousands of years and they are not mans' toy to manipulate as we see fit," Brintkowski said with a timbre in his voice that harkened back to his days behind a lectern.

"I guess, Professor, but I've seen his handiwork and there is no justification for that level of brutality."

"No, I dare say there is not, Mick. But remember, Martin Luther King, Jr only got so far with his 'I have a dream' pacifism before Malcolm X had to take it to the next logical point with a 'By any means necessary' mantra."

Just then Sara returned and we bid the Professor goodbye as we collected our car from valet and I held the door as Sara slid into the passenger seat. Gliding in next to her I ran my hand up her thigh and said, "I believe that your fingers have a standing date with my zipper, Miss Evans."

CHAPTER 21

The next morning I knocked out a couple of columns for the *Insider*. The first was one that I had heavily researched where I compared Law to other notorious serial killers like Ted Bundy, Gary Ridgway, Jeffrey Dahmer and John Wayne Gacy. Law currently was credited with taking 41 lives - Lauren Tate, the helicopter pilot and cameraman, Jack Finch and the 37 poor souls that took a day off of work to go on that fateful Strata-Screamer ride. That ranked him 3rd all time in American history behind Ridgway and the clubhouse leader, Samuel Little. Little was originally convicted of killing three women, but eventually the FBI tied him to 50 murders covering 19 states between the years of 1970 and 2005. Little claims that his actual number of victims is 93 and his FBI investigation is still ongoing.

I concluded my article by saying that what separated Law from the others was that he had a clear motive that wasn't so much tied to his victims as to their connection to a world wonder that he sought to protect and that is what made him dangerous in a way unprecedented in American history. I had Howard Dodson go down to the top of the gorge just past the falls and take a picture of a man's shadow protruding out right to the edge. He captured it even better than I had imagined and I knew we had our cover shot.

The second article detailed the ongoing investigation of a group of rogue cops by the upper brass of the Niagara Falls Police Department. I didn't name Darnell Morgan, or any of the cops for that matter, it was just the first salvo in what I soon hoped would be a bombardment leading to the ouster of the nefarious cops. The article featured a lot of "secret police sources tell me" types of quotes – all of which had come from Sally. The piece was her idea, she wanted to turn up the burner under Morgan and watch him tap dance on the flame for awhile.

Speaking of Sally, just moments later she showed up at my offices.

"Hey, Mick. Do you have a free minute?"

"Of course, Sal. What's up?"

"All's quiet with Law at the moment, but I need to talk with you about something personal."

"Sure, can I get you a drink or anything?"

"No, I'm good. Look I'm going to just come out and say this, I put Lorraine LaFleur on retainer today."

"You did, for what?" I asked, a bit startled at hearing Sal speak the name of Niagara Falls' top divorce attorney.

"Things have gotten worse with Craig. He's more distant than ever and I found some texts that he sent back and forth with some woman named Lucy, a barmaid at that cheeky place with the 1950s theme out on Route 62."

"You don't think he's cheating on you, do you Sal? Craig loves you and the kids."

"No, I don't think he's cheating, but I think he's thought about what his life would be with someone else and he's wondering if we are truly meant to be soul mates. And, to be honest, so have I."

"Sal, I don't know what to say…"

She quieted my words by raising up her hand.

"Look, Mick. I'm not making any rash decisions, but if it does come down to divorce I don't want him to be able to hire Lorraine. She never loses and her clients always get the big end of the wishbone."

Just then, Sally's phone rang.

"It's Carlson," she said before answering it on speakerphone.

"I'm here with Mick O'Malley, Agent Carlson, what…"

Carlson cut her off mid sentence.

"Good, that saves me another call. My agents have Dan Reese in a stand-off at a summer house in Olcott. He's armed and has already fired at officers at the scene. Thank God nobody's been hit. We have a negotiator on scene and Reese is demanding to speak with you, O'Malley. I need you both to get out there now. I'll send you the address."

"We're on our way," Sal responded and terminated the call. "Get ready, Mick. It's time for your closeup."

CHAPTER 22

June 27th

Charlie Grayson could not figure out who was ringing his doorbell so incessantly.

"I knew I should have invested in one of those damned video doorbells," he said aloud as he pulled on some sweatpants and headed toward the Clark Hall wrought iron door that served as the main entranceway to his posh home.

Grayson lived in the desirable Cayuga Creek neighborhood of Niagara Falls. His 2,950 sq ft Colonial two-story home featured 4 bedrooms and 2 ½ baths. It had boat slips with 77-feet of dock space that led out onto Cayuga Creek - a tributary of the upper Niagara River.

Once the house had been filled to the brim with the laughter of the six Grayson children, but that was an era that had now passed. The youngest child, daughter Ashley, had left for college last year and now Charlie and Amelia Grayson were empty nesters. Charlie was just 14 months away from retirement as Chief Plant Manager of Royce Chemical Corporation. He and Amelia had a timeshare in Sarasota that they were hoping to transition from vacation home to retirement residence.

Peering out through the peephole of the door, Grayson saw a man in some kind of uniform holding up what appeared to be an ID badge.

"Hello, sir, My name is Phelps, I'm with NiMo here to check your electrical meter," said the man in a cheerful enough voice.

"You fools read the meter last week," said Charlie Grayson as he unbolted the lock and swung the big door open. "It's no wonder you charge so much for electricity when you double down on unnecessary service call…"

Grayson was cut off mid-rant as he found himself looking down the take no prisoners end of the Desert Eagle nickel-plated .44 that the meter reader stuck in his face.

"Tut, tut that's no way to treat a working stiff like me, Mr. Grayson. Now, why don't you step back into your home nice and slow. Is there anyone else here?"

"No," the startled Grayson answered truthfully. "My wife is out for the day."

"Good, I'm not in the business of harming innocents," said the man as he backed Grayson down onto the off-white Fabio Leather Cinema Sofa that served as the centerpiece of the Plant Manager's living/movie viewing room.

"Hey, I know you. We met at the Mayor's State of the City address, you're…"

 "Silence! Allow me to properly introduce myself, and allow me to apologize for that Phelps nom de plume – seems like the type of fake name someone might conjure up in the moment without investing much effort, I expect better of myself. Despite your knowledge of who I was previously, I'm now the Public Enemy Number 1 they call 'Law,' and I must say, (letting out a long, slow whistle) you do know how to impress with your furniture choices Mr. Grayson. This bad boy is loaded. Speakers, electric recliners, a fridge? Tell me this couch doesn't actually have a built-in fridge now does it?"

Grayson bowed his head before nodding ashamedly in the affirmative.

"Just what do you want with me? I've caused you no harm,"

Grayson said before Law stuck the barrel of the .44 in his mouth.

"I will do the talking if you don't mind. By the way, the gun you are now fellating, the Desert Eagle or Deagle for short, is made to do one thing – put a giant fucking hole in whatever you aim it at. The kind of hole that even skilled surgeons can't sew shut. It's Israeli-made, so you know it won't ever jam like the crap we put out in this country these days. It weighs 4.5 pounds and the combination of it's short-stroke piston, rotating bolt lockup and fixed barrel make it quite unique in the field of guns and ammunitions. In short, Mr. Grayson, if I were to put a white canvas behind your head and pull the trigger we'd have one hell of an abstract art creation. Who knows, the bone fragments of your skull just might get it deemed a multi-media piece?"

Grayson's eyes filled with fear and he opened his mouth to speak, but Law's fearless brain beat him to the draw.

"Don't fret my good man, this gun is far too kind a weapon to use on the likes of you. It's quick and painless while you deserve something, shall we say, a bit more tempered and nuanced. Now, do me a favor and count backwards slowly from five."

Grayson complied, "Five, four, three, two..."

Before he could utter what Harry Nilsson described as the loneliest number, Law pulled the barrel of the pistol from Grayson's mouth and cold-cocked him over the head with it.

It's amazing that human instinct in a moment like this always causes them to be submissive, Law thought,
Watch any nature documentary about the animals of the Serengeti and you'll know that the only way for prey to survive is to fight with all they've got, then run like hell.

"Rise and shine, no friend of mine," Law spoke as Charlie Grayson began to regain consciousness courtesy of the smelling salt stick being waved under his nose.

The Amonium Carbonite vapors in the stick irritated the mucous membranes in the nose and lungs of Charlie Grayson causing the muscles that controlled his breathing to work faster, giving him more oxygen. Slowly his eyes began to open.

"Where am I? What's happening?" Grayson asked as he tried to sit up before realizing that he was duct taped down to the table he was lying on. He also realized, to his horror, that he was nude.

"Where you are, my good man, is inside the old 99th Street school in a part of this fine city now known by the entirely incorrect moniker of Love Canal – nothing lovely about it, not one damn thing," said Law as he stuffed a gag in the stunned man's mouth.

Grayson looked around the abandoned schoolroom and saw that there was an old teacher's desk pulled alongside the table he was on. On it was a vial of orange liquid and something metallic that occasionally glistened as a ray of sunshine coming in from the window reflected off of its surface.

"This school, Mr. Grayson, was once a place of learning. From February 14, 1955 to August 2, 1978, the laughter of class after class of innocent children could be heard reverberating off of the walls of this fine institution. Now, you may wonder why a relatively young 23- year-old school would abruptly shut it's doors, during summer recess no less, might you not, Charlie? Worry not, my good man. I'll tell you why, it was because of the greed of companies like the one that employs you, that's why."

"Buu Myy," Grayson began to protest through his gag.

"Silence!" Law said as he picked up the orange liquid from the table and threw the entire contents of the vial into Grayson's face.

The gag was no match for the scream of pure agony that emitted from the bound man's mouth and echoed throughout the moribund building.

"The immense pain that you are experiencing, Mr. Grayson, is from the unholy combination of hydrochloric and nitrate acids combined in Aqua Regia – the world's most deadly acid. Known as 'Royal Water,' it was developed to dissolve noble metals like gold and platinum. Now I admit throwing it in your face is a blatant misuse of it's intended purpose, but that type of reckless abandon is at the heart of what brings us together here today, don't you agree?"

Grayson was still screaming into his gag in a futile attempt to help relieve the incomprehensible pain he was recoiling in.

"Well, if you were able to think of anyone but yourself right now, you'd agree. You see, Charlie, misuse really should be considered the unofficial 8th Deadly Sin. The land here was originally misused by that snake William Love to build a canal to his ill-fated metropolis situated down below the ridge. Then the city of Niagara Falls saw the children of their soon-never-to-be noble-again city swimming in the canal and decided to misuse their dipping pool as a garbage dumping ground. But that wasn't enough, they soon entered into a financially beneficial agreement to allow a chemical company named after a prostitute – come to think of it they were prostitutes weren't they? The worst kind, the kind that treats entire generations of people as lowly Johns. Well, I digress. The city decided to turn a buck by letting this ungodly company buy the land and dump thousands of tons of some of the worst factory by-product ever created into the ground where their children lived, ate, slept and swam. Then they did something even worse. They decided to build a school, this school on top of all of those buried chemicals."

Grayson's screaming began to die down only because his diaphragm was exhausted from the exertion necessary to wail repeatedly at such decibels.

"Here are the salient numbers, Mr. Grayson. Decades of dumping put over 21,000 tons of chemicals in the ground. When the famed Blizzard of '77 hit, the ground couldn't handle the excess water as the snow melted that spring. Black ooze started seeping up through the ground. Contained within it were over 200 distinct organic chemical compounds, among them were benzene, chloroform, toluene, dioxin, and various kinds of PCB. Bad shit, Mr. Grayson, the kind of shit that your plant is still producing today, but anything for good-paying jobs, isn't that the mantra of your ilk?"

Grayson began screaming again as his diaphragm rallied for a new round of blood-curdlers.

"Scream away, my good man, does my ears good and there's no one left in this once vibrant neighborhood to hear you anyway. Here's the worst part, Charlie. Hooker Chemical knew of the death they were selling to the future generations of Niagara Falls."

Law picked up a book and thumbed to a particular page.

"This is from a correspondence between a Vice President of Hooker and the company President after the VP had consulted with Hooker's legal counsel, one Ansley Wilcox II, concerning the proposed sale of the land from Hooker back to the city: 'The more we thought about it, the more interested Wilcox and I became in the proposition, and finally came to the conclusion that the Love Canal property is rapidly becoming a liability because of housing projects in the near vicinity of our property. A school, however, could be built in the center unfilled section (with chemicals underground). We became convinced that it would be a wise move to turn this property over to the schools provided we could not be held responsible for future claims or damages resulting from underground storage of chemicals.'"

Law paused a moment to let the impact of what he'd just read sink into Charlie Grayson's mind.

"They sold the souls of our children to cover their own carcinogenic-infesting asses. Our children! They knew the ground was rife with chemicals and they decided that building a grade school over it was the best way to minimize their culpability. This wasn't done in some third world country – it was right, fucking here!" Law screamed as he reached over to the table and retrieved the metallic object.

"This, Charlie, is the American Angler PRO fish filleting knife. It is made for precision cuts into soft flesh. It is built for exacting chefs and it will now be used to exact justice."

Grayson began to whimper through his gag.

"When I served in the Army I spent some time in post-war Vietnam. While there I was introduced to a process called Lingchi. It is more commonly known as 'Lingering Death' or 'Death By 1,000 Cuts.' It was borrowed from the Chinese who used it as a form of torture from the seventh century until it was outlawed in 1905. Modern man always has to ruin the classics, doesn't he?"

Law moved down to the end of the table by Grayson's feet. He raised the knife and quickly inflicted a cut on the sole of the horrified man's left foot. Grayson wailed anew.

"That's one, 999 to go," said Law as he inflicted a second cut.

After the 135th cut, which had covered the lower third of his body, Charlie Grayson mercifully passed out. Law reached for the smelling salts stick and waved it under the unresponsive man's nose. After 30 seconds, Charlie Grayson regained consciousness and his mind began to soak in the horror that his nightmare wasn't concluded, but was merely getting started.

"865 cuts to go, my dear Charlie. Rest assured you will be awake for them all."

CHAPTER 23

As Sally pulled her Chevy Impala to the side of the road just up from the summer bungalow that Carlson had directed us to, I had to marvel at the scene unfolded before us. Olcott, New York is a tiny hamlet of about 1,200 people that sits on the shores of Lake Ontario about 28 miles northeast of Niagara Falls. Decades ago it had a bustling beach and a vibrant amusement park that featured the best haunted house ride in the entire state of New York. All of that had fallen apart by the early '80s as the town fell victim to the same economic downturn that had befallen the rest of Niagara County.

These days Olcott had begun a rebuild centered around a much smaller amusement park aimed at young children featuring a handful of classic Herschell amusement rides. The town also played host to a series of successful summer and fall festivals highlighted by the ever-popular Pirate Fest.

What the town had really rebranded itself as was a desirable fishing destination. Anglers travelled from all over to try their hand at hauling in various varieties of fresh water fish like: Walleye, Small and Largemouth Bass, Salmon, Northern Pike and Muskie.

Usually, the town had a slow, easy roll to it. As for crime, there was an occasional domestic dust-up, the odd DWI and the ever lovable report of a cow tipping. That is why what Sally and I drove into was so mind blowing.

The State Police had erected a barricade a mile up the road where we had to show ID to pass. As we exited Sally's vehicle, it looked like we'd stepped into an episode of the old SWAT TV series. There had to be at least 25 vehicles with lights flashing lining the sides of the road. State Troopers, County Sheriffs and Towns of Lockport and Middleport Police all joined FBI vehicles in making it the most exciting day in Olcott recorded history.

As we approached the command post we were waved over by Agent Carlson.

"Reese is in the living room area on the northern side of the house facing Lake Ontario," Carlson explained. "There is poor cellphone coverage so we have been communicating by a throw phone. Melanie Reese is being held as a hostage. We have confirmed that she is unharmed, but Reese has threatened to kill her, then himself if we don't give him what he wants."

"And that would be?" I asked.

"To talk to you alone, O'Malley."

15 minutes later I'd been outfitted with a bulletproof vest and a combat helmet and goggles. I also had a two-way wire strapped to my chest and a nearly undetectable earpiece in my left ear so that Carlson could talk me through the negotiation.

"We're giving you 10 minutes, no more, O'Malley. You will go to within 5-feet of the front door and not a step farther. If you can't get him to surrender within the time limit I'll give a signal and you will retreat immediately. If I sense you are in danger I will pull the plug sooner. Trust your instincts and get out of there if your spider sense starts tingling. We will have 12 of the top snipers in America with scopes trained on him from every possible angle. If he makes any aggressive moves we will take him out," Carlson explained.

"Jesus, somebody explain to me why I went to college for journalism and didn't go into something safer – like lion taming or oil rigging," I joked in a vain effort to calm my pulsating nerves.

"Mick," Sally spoke as she pulled me into an embrace. "Don't play hero ball, you aren't trained for this shit. There's no shame in punting and living for another set of downs."

"Nobody ever named a punter as their favorite player, Sal. Don't worry, I'll be safe, but I'm going to get Dan to give himself up," I said not really believing my words as much as I hoped she would.

I began walking up the driveway towards the house. It was maybe 20 yards, but it felt like I was walking the green mile. Carlson began talking in my ear.

"Put your hands up over you head, O'Malley and keep them there. We don't want him thinking you're armed. When you get to 5 feet from the door, stop and call out to him. No matter what happens do not breach that threshold."

As I took the last few steps before my target point my mind raced back to the years when Dan Reese worked for the *Insider*. He was a college freshman when he started. Grew up in Long Island, like a lot of kids that come to study at Niagara University. He was a wide-eyed innocent then. He wanted to change the world and was naïve enough to think he stood a chance of doing it.

He continued to write columns while he attended law school at the University of Buffalo. Nobody worked harder at a story than he did. One time we got some intel that a huge medical firm was laying off employees and shutting down locations while their upper-level managers were all treating themselves to lavish trips and seven figure bonuses. Dan dug at the layers of their coverup like a squirrel digging for a lost buried nut. He finally was able to get his hands on an internal memo showing that the only reason the company was in the red was because of the mismanagement at the top. We ran the story and a lot of deserving people kept their jobs, while the curdled cream at the top were all let go.

"Okay, O'Malley you're there. Stop and call to him," Carlson commanded in my earpiece.

"Dan, It's Mick. I'm unarmed, is it okay if I put my arms down?"

The door cracked slowly and a broom handle with a woman's compact mirror taped to the end was thrust through the open slot. The mirror angled this way and that as Dan Reese was making sure that there was no ambush awaiting him from either side of the house. Satisfied, the broom handle was retracted and the fallen assistant DA stepped into the doorway.

"Hi, Mick. Long time no see," Reese said as he motioned for me to lower my arms.

"Yeah, lunch over a steak and cheese sub would've been a much easier way to catch up than all of this," I said, trying my best not to let my nerves get the better of me.

"God, I could kill for a Viola's right now," Dan said, referencing Western New York's best sub shop. "My doctor put me on a gluten-free diet last winter. It sucks the big one, Mick."

"I can imagine. Dan, the cops need to know that Melanie is unharmed. Please tell me she's okay."

"You know how much I love her, Mick. I would never hurt her, I just couldn't have her talking to the police until I figure things out. Tell Mick you're okay, Baby," Reese said as he swung the door open wide enough for me to see his wife seated on a couch behind him, her hands duct taped behind her back.

"I'm okay, Mick," Melanie spoke as tears began running from her eyes. "Please tell him to stop this insanity and give himself up."

"Enough!" Reese barked as he turned his back on his sobbing wife. "Happy, Mick?"

"Yeah, thanks. Look Dan, they've got me on a pitch count here, tell me what's going on. Why are we here?"

The assistant DA paused to collect his thoughts and I could see the pain seep out of his brain and trickle across the nerves of his face.

"Lauren Tate, Lauren fucking Tate, that's why we're here, Mick."

"Did you kill her, Dan?"

"Kill her? What kind of a question is that? What about me? She killed me, Mick. That helicopter explosion was too kind for that bitch."

"Get the details, O'Malley," Carlson's disembodied voice spoke in my ear.

"What exactly happened, Dan? Walk me through it."

"It started two years ago when a Hollywood location scout, Fred Ballantine, reached out to my brother, Harold, you know, the bigwig at Falls Real Estate and had him take him around to historic buildings they might use for the Annie Edson Taylor movie they had in preproduction. My brother brought him to see our house and he loved that it was nearly 200 years old and had been updated only within the parameters of keeping it historically correct. We cut a deal to have it used as the home of Annie Taylor's manager in the movie."

"Keep him talking, O'Malley. Anything he says to implicate himself is a bonus," Carlson instructed.

"That sounds like good news, Dan. What made you turn on Lauren Tate?"

"Soon after we signed the deal, Ballantine brought Lauren Tate to town and we all had dinner at our house. She and Mel hit it off famously. Lauren told me that she was shopping for a new personal agent and wanted to look outside of the Hollywood usuals. To make a long story short, we kept communicating and she took a real shine to me. Six months later we entered into an agreement that I would serve as her new representation."

"Again, that all sounds good, Dan," I said as I calculated that we were more than half way through Carlson's deadline for me to bail.

"Yeah, it was better than you can even imagine, Mick. After 'Barrel Queen' she was set to star in the next superhero block-buster, playing a character called 'Hellcat.' I was going to get the standard 10% of her earnings. Do you know how much jack that would have been, Mick? With the movie and the merchandising? Millions, fucking millions."

"So what went wrong, Dan?" I asked.

He stared off in the distance as his eyes looked upward in recollection and his face grew tortured with the memory of a fortune sniffed, but never tasted.

"Everything was all set. Two months ago I put in my notice with the county. We were going to move into a rental during the shoot, then look for a place out in Southern California. My star was ascending, Mick. Then, out of nowhere, I got a letter from the law firm representing United Talent Agency. It said that Lauren Tate had a change of mind and wanted one of their new hotshot agents to handle her career. They'd found a loop-hole in the contract we'd signed and were prepared to exercise it. They offered $100,000 as compensation for my trouble. Can you fucking believe that? A measly hundred grand? If I refused, they planned to get an injunction preventing me from repre-senting her until they could get my contract nullified."

"Jesus," I said knowing that my FBI issued clock was about to strike midnight.

"Yeah, even he couldn't help me, Mick. I tried calling her and she blocked my number. Mel tried and got the same non response. I sent her a letter to try and put the fear of God into her..."

"You didn't have to kill her, you bastard!" Melanie Reese began screaming at her husband. "Or any of the rest of them. You're going to hell, Dan, straight to hell!"

"What are you talking about you crazy bitch? You think she should have gone on living the good life after she left me high and dry?" Reese screamed as he whirled away from me and pulled a Glock that had been concealed in his waistband and aimed the gun at his wife's head.

"Everything I did, I did for you. To provide you with your Mercedes and the house, the jewelry, the vacations - everything Goddamn..."

"Hit the ground, O'Malley, now!" Carlson's voice barked in my ear and my instincts immediately obeyed.

What happened next will haunt me for the rest of my days in this life and well into the nightfalls of the next. I felt a bullet whizz by my ear, followed by two more in rapid succession. Whoosh, whoosh, whoosh. The first hit Dan Reese in the back square between his shoulder blades. The next two blasted into his head. One caught him behind the left ear taking it and the surrounding skull clean off. The second hit the top middle of his head and exploded it like a watermelon dropped off of a skyscraper.

Dan Reese was dead before his body hit the ground. Melanie Reese's face and body were covered in her husband's blood and the gray matter of his brain.

My ears were ringing louder than the church bells of St. Mary's – due both to the aftermath of the speeding bullets and to the echoing wails of a forever-scarred Melanie Reese.

CHAPTER 24

"You sure you're okay, O'Malley? I need you with a clear mind," Agent Carlson asked me as he, Sally and I met in a secured room at police headquarters.

"I'm about as good as I will be," I answered truthfully.

Just 16 hours had passed since a hail of bullets had narrowly missed killing me and had ended Dan Reese's life just inches before my shell-shocked eyes. Melanie Reese was unharmed physically, but the trauma of her ordeal had resulted in her being kept on 24-hour suicide watch on the psych ward of Memorial Medical Center.

Local and national TV crews had been dispatched to the Olcott standoff and had been on a live feed when everything went down. By now, most of the free world had witnessed Dan Reese's execution. The question on everyone's lips was, "Was Law now dead?" That's what the three of us had assembled to try and figure out.

"Good to know," Carlson replied. "Despite the brief remarks I gave to the press last night, we have not made any public statement on the Dan Reese incident. Just to update the two of you, his body was remanded to the morgue and the medical examiner will make an official determination of cause of death later today. All of the agents that discharged their weapons are currently on paid administrative leave as per FBI policy."

"Anything new on Melanie Reese?" Sally asked.

"She's still being monitored. We attempted to get a statement from her, but her doctors are recommending that we wait until her mental condition improves," Carlson answered.

"So where are we in relation to Law?" I asked. "Although, I still can't believe it, it sure sounded like Dan confessed to the Tate murder."

"I tend to agree, O'Malley. The FBI is prepared to announce that we have exacted justice in the murder of Lauren Tate and rule that case closed. We feel that his recorded statements to you were tantamount to a confession and lacking any other credible suspects we feel confident in moving forward in this direction," Carlson responded.

"But what about the other murders? The Strata-Screamers and Jack Finch? Reese didn't mention them at all," Sally demanded.

"No, unfortunately Mrs. Reese's goading of her husband caused a premature ending of O'Malley's questioning of Reese, but we believe that he would have confessed to those killings also," Carlson retorted.

"Jesus, are we really blaming Melanie Reese for that shit show of an outcome, yesterday? You guys have the best hostage negotiators in the world on your payroll and you put Mick's life in danger by sending him in alone and now you blame the woman when it all goes sideways? You take the fucking cake, Carlson."

"Watch your sharp tongue, Miss Wendt."

"It's Mrs. Wendt," Sally cut him off. "And I understand your agents saved a woman's life yesterday, but let's not lose sight of what put it in danger in the first place."

"Noted," Carlson conceded. "To get back on point, we need to develop a firm position and present it to the press as a united front."

Two hours later Carlson, Sally and I were sharing a podium on a platform positioned in front of police headquarters. They had shut down Main Street for two blocks in either direction to make room for the plethora of news outlets from all points on the globe that had turned out to get all of the gory and lurid details on the downing of America's most notorious mass murderer. Looking out I couldn't help but be bewildered by what had become of my small tourist city.

"Ladies and Gentlemen of the press, my name is FBI Special Agent Keith Carlson and on behalf of all of the law enforcement personnel present we thank you for joining us on this somber, yet relief-providing, day. It is my duty to report to you that at precisely 2:12 PM yesterday afternoon agents of the Federal Bureau of Investigation inflicted three high-powered rifle shots to the person of Daniel Bartholomew Reese, one of which proved fatal. Furthermore, it has been concluded that Mr. Reese was indeed the federal suspect known as 'Law' who has been terrorizing the surrounding communities for the past month and who is credited with the taking of 41 souls."

A hailstorm of questions came flying forth from the assembled press corps - the likes of which are often dramatized in movies, but rarely seen in real life. Carlson was nonplussed as he quieted the crowd.

"Now, now, now we will take your questions at the conclusion of the briefing, but first I need to take you through the events that led up to yesterday's stand-off," Carlson said and then proceeded to do just that.

When he'd finished he opened the proceedings up for questioning. He and Sally adroitly handled a bevy of questions from the national media powerhouses. Just when it looked like things were about to wrap up and I could go somewhere dark and quiet for a long, long time, my old nemesis, Jeffery Lordes of the *Morning News* forced his way to the forefront and screamed out my name.

"Mick, Mick O'Malley, Jeffery Lordes of the award-winning *Niagara Falls Morning News* here," the self-promoting blowhard blurted out. "Mick, how does it make you feel to know that your former protégé, Dan Reese, has been proven to be one of America's most prolific serial killers? Do you feel that his time at your sleazy *Insider* set him on that path and do you feel some culpability for his murderous spree?"

Time froze. I felt a stunned hush go over the crowd of reporters in reaction to Lordes' ridiculously inappropriate questions. I felt the blood momentarily drain from my head and then, in an instant, the thousands of years-in-the-making Irish DNA that ran through my veins kicked in and I reacted in a way that my forefathers would have applauded.

I leapt from the podium, fists clenched, and headed straight for the arrogant prick. His eyes opened up and got as wide as frisbees. Still, he stayed rooted like a deer caught in the high beams.

"You cocksucker!" I yelled as my right fist make contact with the left side of his no longer smug face.

He dropped to the ground as Sally and a small band of Niagara Falls Police officers tackled me and took me to the cement alongside him. I could hear flashbulbs popping and camera shutters whirring as the national media couldn't believe that the sublime had just gone to the ridiculous.

For them it was an insane scene, but, even in my enraged state, I knew it was just another sunny day for Niagara Falls.

CHAPTER 25

Three days had passed since Dan Reese was shot dead right in front of me and you could call me anything but okay. Carlson, Sally and I had all independently appeared on every TV network from coast to coast. I had put together an edition of the *Insider* dissecting the case from every angle. The cover featured a picture of Dan Reese at his Assistant DA swearing in ceremony, with an inset of his dead body being taken away from the Olcott house on a gurney. The headline read, "We Fought the Law and Nobody Won."

Carlson and his FBI team were conducting a summary and conclusion of the Law case and would, presumably, be leaving town soon to track down the next top-priority lunatic. It was announced that there would be a huge memorial service in Hollywood to pay tribute to the life of Lauren Tate and the two men that died on the helicopter with her. It had been held up while Law was still on the loose as her family did not want his shadow looming over the affair.

I had only seen Sally once since everything went down and that was when she tackled me to save me from beating Jeffery Lordes half to death. Fortunately, the parent group that owned the *Morning News* was so embarrassed by their writer's lack of professional acumen that they refused to press assault charges against me. The whole sordid affair was now like the season of *Dallas* before Bobby stepped out of the shower – everyone saw it, but it didn't really happen.

Sally had texted me a few times to keep me in the loop of the case aftermath. It appeared that she would get a promotion within the police department as she was the darling of the public's eye and for that I was very happy.

Yet, something didn't feel right to me. There was ambiguity in Dan Reese's words to me just before he was killed. I've lived long enough to know that you can never trust ambiguity. When something is right, it's almost always concrete. This case should have ended with a big bow tied up all around it, instead there were just a lot of loose strings.

Why did Dan feel that he had to kill Lauren Tate? How did he get access to her helicopter? Why did he kill so many tourism professionals at Aquatic World? Dan always espoused the benefits of tourism dollars in sustaining the city. Why was Jack Finch defiled in such a heinous manner? Dan had a beautiful wife and two lovely and amazing daughters, why would he throw that all away? Could a man with such a busy professional and personal life even have the time to plot and carry out so many murders?

None of it made any sense and it felt like my brain was attempting to solve a Rubik's Cube featuring every nuanced color on the spectrum. To make matters worse, Sara had taken it upon herself to move into my place to take care of me in my time of need. I'd have rather signed up for a colonoscopy performed by a sadist. She was smothering me and my drug of choice was quickly becoming the thought of breathing some fresh, cool air.

I sat on my couch with my eyes closed and tried to shake the feeling that Dan Reese wasn't meant for the paintbrush that history was aiming to color him with. I kept replaying the scene of his shooting over and over in my head. I labored over every word I'd spoken to him. I kept wishing that I could conjure up a string of words that would have led to a different outcome, one where my longtime friend wouldn't have been shot down like a rabid wolf in front of his beautiful wife. I tried and I tried, but that word chain just wouldn't form. Every time I felt close to a reply to something Dan had said that would lead to a non-violent ending the triple whoosh would sound in my ears and in the next instant I would see Dan Reese's head explode like a piñata cracked with a solid oak stick.

"Daddy, you'd feel a whole lot better if you took me in the bedroom and pounded me like a scaloppine," Sara said in an attempt to break me out of my depression. "You can even knock on the back door if you like."

Now there are crossroads in one's life that age and experiences just sort of naturally deposit you at. I found myself at just such a desolate intersection at that very moment. There I was with a beautiful, sultry woman basically telling me that her body was an amusement park that I had an all-access pass to. She was telling me that a life lived with her would be one of untold sexual excesses. It would be one where she would always willingly offer up her feminine charms as a portal to teleport me away from my misery. She was nearly any red-blooded heterosexual man's dream come true. At one time, not so long ago, she was mine, too. But that ship had sailed, Law had seen to that.

"What in the hell is wrong with you?" I screamed in the type of voice that would immediately make a woman reach into her purse and get her hands on that can of pepper spray that she'd hoped she'd never have to use.

"Mick? What's wrong?" Sara asked with no clue as to how I was going to answer.

"You, you're what's wrong, Sara. Jesus fucking Christ, can't you comprehend what I'm going through? Some lunatic has been killing innocent people and using me as his mouthpiece. The police thought it was Dan Reese, Goddamn Dan Reese, and they shot him dead right in front of me, nearly sending my sorry ass to the pearly gates right along with him."

"Mick, I…"

NIAGARA FALLS INTO DARKNESS

"Don't Mick me you nutty bitch. You think every problem in the world can be solved by offering up your body? It can't! What I need, have needed for a long time in fact, is for you to be an adult. Not some woman/child still acting out sexually over something that happened to you when you were five."

"How dare you!" Sara screamed, tears flowing out of her eyes in a sudden dam burst. "I trusted you with my past, I don't need you wielding it like an axe to cut my heart open."

"Oh, save me the waterworks and the dramatics, Sara. If you could only spread joy with the same gusto that you spread your legs, maybe you'd be of some use to me."

And that was the straw that broke Sara Evan's flexible back.

"I'm done, Mick. Done, do you hear me? I've given you everything and you've done nothing, but string me along," Sara screamed as she grabbed her purse and headed for the door. "Don't even think about calling me, Mick. You just threw away the best thing that you'll ever have."

A wave of remorse immediately swept over me. I grabbed her by the arm and held tight.

"Sara, look. I'm sorry. I didn't mean that, any of it. I really haven't been fair to you. You're amazing and you deserve so much better," I said, meaning every word.

"Well, we finally agree on something," Sara spat as she broke free from my grip. "I do deserve so much better than you."

A quick whirl and door slam later and I found myself in a place that sadly was no stranger to me – all alone.

CHAPTER 26

What's that old chestnut from The *Godfather III?* "Just when I thought I was out, they pull me back in!"

It was 8 AM on a Thursday morning, the second day PS – post Sara. I was eating an everything bagel with cream cheese and drinking a supercharged cup of coffee when there was a banging on my door that would have awoken the deadest of the dead. I looked through my peephole to see the face of a ginger goddess who went by the Earthly name of Sally. In the few seconds it took me to unbolt my door I tried to decide if she looked anxious, angry, excited or bored. I couldn't come to any solid conclusion, but I did make a mental note never to sit down at a poker table with her.

"Come on Mick, open the damn door," Sally said a nanosecond before I accomplished just that.

"I don't move so fast this early," I replied as my tongue swept away the last vestiges of cream cheese clinging to the corner of my mouth. "What brings you by at this ungodly hour?"

"You should probably sit down, Mick."

"Why?" I asked as I complied while I felt my muscles tense for the sure-to-be startling words that always follow that request.

"Dan Reese wasn't Law. Law's still out there and he's taken another victim," Sally said.

"What? Who? What are you saying to me, Sal?"

"The Lieutenant working the overnight desk took a call around

4 AM. Male caller, burner phone with an untraceable number and he disguised his voice with an app. The guy said he was Law. He said that he had enjoyed watching us make fools of ourselves by stating that Dan Reese was him and by calling the case closed. He said we should check out the old 99th Street school and we should bring the forensic team with us along with a body bag."

"This is surreal, Sal. What happened when you got there?"

"We found what was left of one Charlie Grayson."

"The guy from Royce Chemical?"

"Yeah, do you know him?" Sal asked.

"Not well, but he sat at a table with Johnny Guts and I at a Rotary meeting last year. Nice guy, I talked him up a bit and his company ended up picking up the tab for a
series of full page ads in the *Insider* that touted the after school programs offered by the Boys and Girls Club. Why would Law target him?"

"Because he blames the chemical companies for polluting the waters of the Niagara River. He left a note to you, in his familiar style, detailing everything. Mick, do you know what Lingchi is?"

"Death by 1,000 Cuts? Sal, no, please tell me that's not what happened to Charlie Grayson?'

"I'm afraid so, Mick. It was even more heinous than the Jack Finch murder scene."

"Christ almighty. So we're right back in this again? Carlson?"

"He's remobilizing his team. We'll be holding a presser at noon today, telling the world that we had the wrong guy and the public needs to stay on high alert."

"That's going to go over like a lead zeppelin. Who are the suspects now?" I asked.

"There are none. We're back at square one. He did offer up a clue as to what may be coming, though."

"How's that?" I asked.

"His note ended with these words, 'The first cut may be the deepest, O'Malley, but the last will blow you away.'"

CHAPTER 27

There was a time when one awaited the evening newspaper to find out what was holding the world's interest. Before that, a town crier would have alerted the populace to what piece of news they should be paying close attention to. But we live in different times and I found out just how surreal they can be the morning after Sal's visit and stunning Clemens-like revelation that the reports of Law's death were indeed greatly exaggerated.

I opened up my iPad and checked in with Twitter to see what was happening in the world. Under "Trending" was the following listing:

1) Global Warming
2) Law YouTube Video
3) President Tweets Criticizing GOP Senator
4) J-Lo's Outfit Blows Up the Internet
5) Mick O'Malley

I felt my heart make like a Maserati as it began to accelerate at a breakneck sped inside of my chest cavity. My fingers began to tremble with the rhythm of Buddy Rich on the hi-hat during his impossible drum solo as I typed "YouTube" into the menu bar and saw Law's video featured at the top of the marquee. It had been up for just over two hours and had already eclipsed over 1,000,000 views.

I got up and fixed myself a cup of coffee and paced around the room for a good 20 minutes before I sat back down and picked up the iPad. I felt like a kid in middle school praying for a snowstorm to close school on the day of a math final. Ultimately, I knew that I would have to find out what the lunatic had to say, but I was somehow holding out hope for divine intervention to at least stave off the inevitable. I finally took a deep breath and touched my index finger to the screen.

"Well, hello. Surprised? You shouldn't be. Dan Reese? Really? I'm beyond offended that anyone would think that halfwit could have been me. Don't you idiots watch 'The Masked Singer?' The first guess is always wrong – and the second and third for that matter," Law began.

He was wearing one of those face-obscuring, unnervingly expressionless masks, sort of like that character in "V for Vendetta." The mask had a small round hole cut in it in the center of the lips. Law was sitting on a chair in a dimly lit room. He was wearing a dark sweatshirt and was shot only from the shoulders up. He had on a pair of off-white driving gloves, the type often sported by NASCAR drivers. His voice was again obscured using a disguise app. There was a white sheet hanging behind him, nothing could be seen of the room to offer law enforcement any clues. He was, in three words, "super fucking creepy" and I had to resist the urge to close the screen and never get on the internet again.

"Let's get the formalities out of the way, shall we? I am the man that lesser men call Law. The one and the only, accept no substitutes. When I go out it will be at a place and time of my choosing, not at some summer shanty out in buttfuck Olcott," Law said as he waved his arms around for extra emphasis.

"I keep hearing and reading so many things that curious minds want to know about me. Tops of course is, 'Who is he?' Well, you'll have to wait for that little reveal my adoring public. Rest assured that you will have that knowledge in the not-so-distant future and from that moment on my name will go down as the greatest citizen ever to call Niagara Falls home," Law said as his computer altered voice made his narcissism seem all-the-more sinister.

"A close second is the question, 'Why is he doing this?' That, my loyal sycophants, is the topic that I am going to cover today. I realize that the majority of you viewing this were reared under the Judeo-Christian teachings, but I think that the people that you stole this land from, the Native Americans, have it right. You see, they believe that we all share one true mother – Mother Earth – and that you must respect, nurture and honor your mother above all things," Law spoke as he fished a pack of his beloved unfiltered Camel cigarettes out of his pocket and lit one up.

"America as a whole, and Niagara Falls in particular, have treated our dear mother with disrespect reflecting the cold and blind hearts that beat inside of bastards that warrant their own abandonment. Think of it, our Mother gave us life on the banks of one of her true wonders. Life-sustaining, calm-inducing, art-inspiring, senses-revitalizing water pouring over the rocks in a never-ending torrent of true magic. And what do we do with that amazing gift?"

"We build factories on it's shoreline and dump untold amounts of chemicals into the water – water that our children drink, for God and Mother's sake. We pollute the air around this nat-ural beauty with smokestacks that run 24-hours a day. We build high rises all around it, detracting from its allure. We run boats up and down the river below it, destroying the shoreline and robbing the generations to come of the opportunity to revel in beauty that we were too blind to see."

Law stuck the tip of the cigarette into the hole and took a long drag on it before continuing on.

"For most of my life, decade after decade, I sat idly by, as all of you have done, and waited for government to do something. 'Surely, they'll clean things up,' I said. But they didn't. Things just kept getting worse. The city around the falls has decayed before my eyes. All of our brightest and most accomplished children have long ago moved away, pushed out by their parents with words to the affect of, 'You need to get out of this city. There's no more opportunity here, everything is gone.' While the population dwindled the poverty rate rose, as did the cancer rates – to levels that lead the nation."

"Where are we today? That's a question that I asked myself for years and then finally had to face the sad, stark truth. Nowhere, we are n-o-w-h-e-r-e!" Law said as he eerily blew a long line of smoke out of the hole in his mask. "So, I decided that the savior I was waiting on was actually the one staring back at me from my bathroom mirror and I devised a plan to get us all back on the right path."

"Now there is an ancient Ashiwi prayer-song that says:

That our earth mother may wrap herself
In a four-fold robe of white meal [snow]; ...
When our earth mother is replete with living waters,
When spring comes,
The source of our flesh,
All the different kinds of corn
We shall lay to rest in the ground with the earth mother's
living waters,
They will be made into new beings,
Coming out standing into the daylight of their Sun father, to all
sides
They will stretch out their hands..."

"You see, the prayer teaches us that our Earth mother draws her power from living waters and there is no water more alive than those that plunge over Niagara Falls. The prayer then goes on to say that those that are laid to rest in the ground with the living water will be reborn into new, more evolved beings." Law said as he used the tapping out of his cigarette as a caesura for his soliloquy.

"So that is why Lauren Tate had to be laid in the ground. She represented the worst word ever associated with Niagara – exploitation. The character she was going to play, Annie Edson Taylor, was the first daredevil that tried to exploit Niagara Falls for personal fame and gain. She wasn't the last. They keep coming like moths to the flame, despite the fact that the falls either kills them or sends them back into the world no more famous or richer for their trouble. I mean, you've never turned on *Jeopardy* and heard someone say, 'I'll take famous Niagara Daredevils for $1,000, Alex,' have you?" Law said and then cackled at his own cleverness.

"It's why Jack Finch had to die, too. He lined his pockets while he destroyed our shoreline. Bubble, bubble, I ended his toil and trouble. Same for that group of idiots on the Strata-Screamer. Green tourism is the only kind that should be practiced here, not the rape and pillage type that their ilk have exercised on the banks of our majestic river." Law said as he stood for dramatic effect, revealing an all-dark outfit of nondescript clothing.

"And it is especially why Charlie Grayson had to, if you'll pardon the pun, have his life cut short. Chemical pollution has been the worst atrocity ever committed against our famed cataracts. Imagine filling your dear children's bathtubs with warm water then adding in a dose of arsenic or PCB for good measure. Unthinkable, right? Yet, it happened here on a widespread scale for decades and the chemical companies and our own useless government smiled as they cashed their checks and sentenced our children to die."

"So, what now you ask? It's a fair question and I will at least offer a clue or two to the answer. By now most of you know that I have used newspaperman Mick O'Malley as my primary form of communication. That choice was not made haphazardly as O'Malley has been a pawn that I have been expertly maneuvering around the chess board from the beginning. So let me speak to him directly: O'Malley you are not just a spectator in this game, you are a player and you are a problem. You could have used your newspaper – you know the one with Niagara Falls as two of the three words in it's title? – you could have used it as a great sword to help cut down the desecration of Niagara Falls, but you instead chose to use it as nothing more than a crane to dump piles of money into your unworthy pockets.

The checkmate is near, Mick. You will help me topple the king and let's just say you'll have a real blast in doing so. William Penn once said, 'People are more afraid of the laws of man than of God, because their punishment seems to be nearest.' I am Law, O'Malley, and your punishment is like objects in the rear view mirror - closer than you think."

CHAPTER 28

Have you ever taken a defensive driving class? If you have you'll know that there is a weird phenomenon that kicks in around hour four of the six-hour course. At that point your brain begins to believe that the first and foremost responsibility in your life is to take every precaution to always be a safe and defensive driver. You actually convince yourself that you will forevermore do things like walk around your vehicle and make a full visual inspection prior to each time you fire up the ignition. You believe that you will routinely check the air pressure in your tires before the little yellow light with the exclamation point tells you to. You swear to yourself that you will stop rolling through stop signs and cutting through parking lots all willy-nilly. By the time they issue that insurance premium reducing certificate you fully believe that you are the safest driver to hit the roads since that little old lady from Pasadena and you can't wait to become a role model for the untrained masses.

Then you step out into the crisp air and suddenly remember that it's not October 1, 1908 and the first Model T hasn't just hit the roadways and driving isn't some Sunday passion affordable only to the upper echelon. You suddenly remember that we in the modern world drive like we make a piece of toast – perfunctory and without any true conscious thought. And you jump in your car and drive the same way that you did before you spent two Saturdays enrolled in automotive adult education.

That's a long way to go to make a point about my state of mind in the days following the release of Law's YouTube video. At first I was all Law all the time. I obsessed on his next move:

Where would it be? What would it be? Would I be the target? But then something happened that ripped me back to reality and made me realize that I could not be a moon orbiting around Law and that there were other gravitational pulls demanding my attention.

My phone rang and I looked at the screen and saw the name Manuela Morgan pop up on the screen.

"Manuela, Hi. What's up?" I asked.

"Mick, thank God. It's Ayesha, he finally did it. We're at St. Mary's, can you come right away?" Manuela spoke in a panic-stricken voice.

"What did Morgan do, Manuela? Please tell me she's going to be okay."

"He brought her home from his visitation yesterday. The left side of her face by her eye was badly swollen. He said she tripped and fell into the door frame. Overnight the swelling only worsened. You couldn't even see her eye. On the drive here she lost consciousness. She's been in with the doctors for nearly 4 hours. They're doing an emergency operation to ease swelling on her brain. Mick, please come I'm scared for my baby."

"I'm on my way, hang tight." I said.

I hopped in my car and headed north toward St. Mary's Hospital. Situated 15 minutes away from downtown Niagara Falls, the hospital is part of the Catholic Health system and is favored by many residents of the area. I parked in the area adjacent to the emergency room reserved for ambulances and lowered my visor displaying my press credentials issued by the county sheriff's office.

I rushed inside and found a distraught Manuela Morgan clutching a wad of Kleenex.

"Manuela," I said as I pulled her into a hug. "Any word on Ayesha's condition?"

"No, they are operating now. Please Jesus, it's not my baby's time, please let her wake up okay."

"I'm praying with you, Manuela. Ayesha's a tough cookie, she's going to be fine. I just know it." I said as I tried to find the comfort in my words that I hoped Manuela would find.

Nearly another two hours passed before we were approached by a silver-haired gentleman in green surgical scrubs.

"Excuse me, Mrs. Morgan? I'm Doctor Grimaldi. I just want to give you an update. We operated on Ayesha to repair a broken orbital bone around her left eye, a detached retina and bleeding on the occipital lobe of the brain. We were able to stem the bleeding and reattach the retina. The orbital bone will require further reconstructive cosmetic surgery. We have put her in an induced coma as a precautionary method. Her life is no longer in danger, but it is possible that she will permanently lose vision in her left eye."

"Sweet Jesus, my poor baby," Manuela exclaimed before collapsing in my arms.

"Doctor, Hi, I'm Mick O'Malley a friend of Manuela. Ayesha's father said she fell into a door frame, is that consistent to what you found when you operated?"

"It's possible. It's the type of injury most commonly seen in boxing as the result of a knock-out punch. It was excessive force trauma, that's a certainty. Beyond that, I'm not comfortable in making a specific determination as to the cause."

"When can I see my baby?" asked Manuela.

"Shortly, Mrs. Morgan. We just want to make sure that her vitals are stable, then we'll bring you back. Thank God you got her here when you did, any longer and we might not have had such a favorable outcome," explained Dr. Grimaldi.

"Where she at? Where's my baby girl?" a uniformed Darnell Morgan asked as he came barreling in through the ER doors.

"You get the hell out of here, Darnell. You did this to her you bastard!" Manuela screamed.

"Bitch, you trippin'. Don't trifle me, I said, where's Ayesha?" Darnell demanded.

"Excuse me, Sir, but may I ask just who you are?" Dr. Grimaldi interjected.

"I'm Ayesha's daddy that's who I am," Darnell responded as he flashed his badge for good measure. "Now, this is the last time I'm gonna ask politely, where in the hell is my daughter?"

"She's in post-op in a coma. You did this to her didn't you Morgan?" I said through clenched teeth.

"What business is it of yours you cracker son-of-a-bitch? I ain't asked you but shit. So kindly fuck off and let me handle my business up in here."

"Ayesha's mother asked me to be here, that's what business of mine it is and I asked you a question, did you strike Ayesha?" I demanded.

"Bitch, Ima 'bout to strike your vanilla ass. Now step off and that's a police order."

"Now, now gentlemen. This is a hospital, I demand that you conduct yourselves with the proper amount of decorum," Dr. Grimaldi said in an attempt at playing peacemaker.

"You want to take this outside, Morgan?" I asked, hotter than a penny on the sidewalks of Tucson, Arizona.

"Yeah, you're damn right I do," Darnell replied as he charged back outside into the ER parking lot.

I followed close on his heels as Manuela Morgan ran behind yelling for us both to stop.

"Why did you hit Ayesha, Morgan?" I said once we were outside and standing face-to-face two feet apart from one another. "Maybe you'd like to take a poke at me tough guy. I promise you I won't be the one needing medical attention once it's over."

"You crazy, O'Malley, you know that? Ayesha tripped and hit the door frame just like I told her moms. And don't think I don't know that you and Sally Wendt aren't tryin' to take me down. You think you gonna play me like that?"

"Mick, please, don't engage him..." Manuela said before I shushed her with a wave of my hand.

"Take you down, Morgan? Yeah, that's a stone cold promise. You're dirty and you're going to take a fall sooner rather than later. More than that, you're a ball-less punk. I've got no respect for any man that hits women and children," I said as I stepped one foot closer to him. "I promise you this, I'm going to see to it that this little girl and her mother are protected from you and when the right time comes I'm going to give you the ass kicking that your daddy should have – badge or no badge."

Morgan's nostrils flared with anger and I thought he was going to charge me. *Come on you bastard, give me proper cause to open up a can of whoop ass on you,* I thought as I quickly strategized how I would handle his attack before counterpunching him into unconsciousness.

Instead, he smiled and took two steps back while putting his hands up just above his shoulders.

"Not today, my man. Manuela, you tell my baby her daddy loves her. You fuckin' with the wrong black man, O'Malley. Don't sleep with both eyes shut, the boogie man comin'" Morgan said before he turned and got into his police cruiser.

"Yeah, well when he does I'll tell him my nickname – Dream Catcher," I yelled as he squealed past me out of the driveway.

"You okay, Mick?" Manuela asked as she clasped my hand for comfort.

"Yeah, Just disappointed. I was ready to throw down with him. Come on, let's go back and check on Ayesha."

CHAPTER 29

Dichotomy, that's a word that I've been thinking about a lot lately. A division or contrast between two things that are or are represented as being opposed or entirely different. Seems to be the definition of my life these past many months. On one hand there is Law, pure evil incarnate. A man so filled with hatred that he is willing to kill to try to prove his point to the world at large. On the other side of that was Manuela Morgan, a woman using every fiber of her maternal instincts to protect her only child from a man nearly as evil as Law.

Then there's the *Insider,* a dichotomy in and of itself. For so long it had been about churning out a buck. Write salacious stories that drive the circulation, use the circulation numbers to generate the ad revenue, use the ad revenue to support my lifestyle. Lather, rinse, repeat.

Recently, however, the Law developments and Darnell Morgan have reminded me why I was drawn to journalism in the first place. There was a great responsibility that came with upholding the rights guaranteed in the First Amendment. I was drawing a sense of pride in helping keep the public aware and informed of Law's thoughts and actions. I was drawing even more from doing whatever I could to protect Ayesha Morgan and her mother from a cop breaking the laws he was sworn to uphold.

Of course, there was also my love life or the remnants thereof. On one side of the coin was Sara. Young, beautiful, sexually available, but really just an empty fortune cookie. Sure, I missed her, but it's always that way when relationships end, especially when you shoulder all of the blame. You miss the familiarity that you had. The food you ate together and the restaurants you frequented, the TV shows you binged while snuggled together on the couch, the songs that defined your union, the inside jokes that made you laugh and made others wonder just what was so damned funny. Sara was gone and there was a hole, but I was sure that I'd made the right decision.

Then there was Sally. The yin to Sara's yang. Sally was wise where Sara was obtuse. She was strong where Sara was weak. She was learned where Sara was green. And she was beautiful, in the truest and deepest measure of that word, where Sara was merely a shiny dust jacket surrounding a book with blank pages. But she was also married and even though that marriage seemed to be on shaky ground, I didn't think that I should be the gust of wind that finally took it down.

All things were black and white in my world now and I was yearning for a real splash of gray.

I was contemplating these matters sitting at my desk at the *Insider* when I received a text from Manuela. Ayesha's vitals had improved and they had brought her out of the induced coma. Sally had helped her secure a restraining order against Darnell and had opened up a formal investigation into the cause of Ayesha's injuries. It was requested that Darnell be put on paid administrative leave pending the outcome of the investigation, but the police union fought it and he had so far avoided suspension. Still, a little gray never felt so good.

Just then Johnny Guts came in and flopped down on the couch across from my desk.

"How you holding up. Mick?"

"I've been better, Johnny. Just found out that Ayesha Morgan is out of her coma though. So that's something to be happy about,"

I answered.

"That is great news. Did they arrest Morgan for it, yet?"

"No, but Sally helped get a restraining order on him and opened up a formal investigation."

"She's a real peach, Mick. Why don't you jump on that bus now that you're a free man?"

"A free man that prefers free women, Johnny. Are we okay for ad sales for the next issue?"

"Yeah, 90% closed. I'm only waiting on Supermarket Liquors to sign-off on the back cover. If they don't commit we can run the one for that not-for-profit, but it's half the revenue and I know you don't want that," Johnny replied.

"Whatever, money isn't everything."

"Whoa, who are you and what have you done with Mick O'Malley? Money isn't everything? Did you hit you head or something?"

"No, I'm just a bit off my game I guess," I conceded.

"I'll say. Anyway, about next issue, you're going to have to put it out without me," Johnny said.

"Why?"

"My mother took a fall a couple of days ago. My sister's been there, but she has her own family to care for. So, I'm going to drive up to Ballston Lake and stay with her for the next week or so. Hopefully, she'll get better, but if not I'll look into getting a home health aide for her."

"Sure, no worries. If there's anything I can do, just let me know. You know I think the world of Helen," I said.

"Thanks. She always asks about you, Mick. Tells me I should be more like you."

"Don't listen to her, Johnny. Moms always have a blind spot and I'm Helen's."

"You got that right. Hey, check this out, I got a new tattoo," Johnny Guts said as he pulled up his left sleeve to reveal an ink portrait of a balding, elderly man with a long flowing beard and mustache.

"Who is that, Plato?" I asked.

"Seriously, Mick? It's Olmsted. The spitting image of him, too. I had it done at that place out on Buffalo Avenue where all the bikers get their's done."

"What made you get your first tattoo now? Midlife crisis? I queried.

"No, well maybe. Just felt right, you know?"

"I guess, but why someone as obscure as a landscape artist?"

"Hey, one man's landscape artist is another man's muse. It just spoke to me, so I went for it."

"God bless, Johnny. I expect you'll come back from Ballston Lake with a nose ring." I chided.

"No, it'd just be one more thing I'd have to remove when I go through the metal detectors over at police headquarters or at the County Courthouse," Johnny said as he got up and headed for the door. "Oh, and Mick, take what Law said on that video seriously, I'd hate to have to start all over with a new partner."

CHAPTER 30

I spent the next few hours after Johnny left organizing the next edition of the *Insider.* We had a small stable of writers and they were all way too talented to be plying their trade for a small city weekly like ours. That was the status of the current newspaper biz, though. Dwindling readership of all things paper – books, magazines and newspapers – had left an over abundance of quality writers with no profitable outlets for their creative output. Millennials didn't read anything if it wasn't on their phones and even then venerable news outlets like *Time, Newsweek and the New York Times* had fallen out of favor, replaced by websites with dubious names like *Mashable, Buzzfeed and Upworthy.*

I figured the *Insider* had only one or two more years putting out print editions. The demographic that enjoyed the tactile experience of holding a newspaper in their hands were quickly moving out of Niagara Falls and into nearby graveyards. The *Morning News* was fighting the same battle. Ironically, it was the revenue generated from obituaries that was keeping them afloat. It used to be the classifieds that brought in the most money, but some guy named Craig and his damned list put an end to that.

Being able to sense the end of the paper era is what had driven me to focus on the *Insider's* online edition ahead of the curve of other print publications. Aside from our focus on local stories I always had one or two of our columnists pen a story featuring a national angle. One week one of our scribes, Chickie Crossvalley, submitted a column about people fascinated that they could stand their brooms upright, thinking it was some once-a-year phenomenon. I told him he was nuts and to submit another piece. Chickie asked me if he'd ever turned in a lemon in his many years with the paper? I told him that he hadn't and he said, "then trust me." So I did. 1.2 million clicks later and $1,000 richer courtesy of Google Adsense and I was a believer.

Just as I finished the final layout of the print edition Sally walked through the door holding a tray with two Tim Horton's cups dressed for travel.

"Hey Mick. I thought your misery might love my company."

"My joy loves your company, too, but I haven't experienced a whole lot of that lately."

"Tell me about it," Sal said as she handed me a cup of dark roast. "Just came by to tell you that Morgan is one slippery bastard. Despite the watch they have him under and despite the knowledge that he presumably nearly killed his daughter, the Chief still has him on active duty."

"Jesus, why? What does he have to do before he's stripped of his badge?" I asked.

"Patience, that's what I keep telling myself, just a little patience. He'll make one wrong move too many, then I'll nail him to the goddamned wall. In the meantime, I've got a crew of cops that I trust most keeping watch on Manuela's house. She filed a restraining order against him for both herself and Ayesha. He's got parental rights, but he'll have to go to family court to get green lit to see Ayesha. If he shows up at the house before then my guys will take him down and OPS will take care of him from there."

I shook my head for a good 20 seconds, experiencing something that I'd heard others speak of, but rarely experienced myself – words failed me.

"How are things with Craig?" I said in an attempt to steer the subject in any other direction. "What's Lorraine LaFleur telling you?"

"Things are worse. He's actually been staying with his brother for the past few days. Lorraine says that if I'm going to file now would be a good time, abandonment and all that."

"Aw, Sal. I'm so sorry. With all that you have on your plate right now, that's the last thing that you need," I offered.

"Yeah, it sucks. The kids are scared. I keep telling them that mommy and daddy love them and that will never change. I don't know, Mick. Sometimes I convince myself that I need to stay until Beth graduates high school, but that's eight years away. Plus that's the kind of crap that every broken woman always says to me just before I call CPS to take her kids away. I'm a lot of things, but a victim isn't one of them."

"I'm here for you, Sal. Just name it and it's done. I'm sure the right answer will come to you soon."

"It'd better. Lorraine charges $300 per hour and with each phone call, meeting and correspondence I'm going through that money like a hot knife through butter."

We were interrupted by a loud buzz from my cellphone.

"It's from Brintkowski. Looks like a group text to Johnny Guts, as well" I said and then read the message aloud.

"Mick/Johnny, there is a ceremony planned aboard the Niagara Falls Boat Ride this coming Friday at Noon. The Greenway Commission will be giving them our President's Award in recognition of their launching All-Electric boats. Governor Macy will be there as well. I'd like you two to be my personal guests. Please RSVP. Regards, John B."

"Man, doesn't he know texting shorthand? His thumbs must ache," Sal joked.

"The man is nothing if not formal," I said.

"I'll be there, too. Captain wants his A-Team there to backup the Governor's security team," Sal said.

"Great. Maybe afterwards we can have our picture taken in one of those 'going over the falls in a barrel' backdrops," I joked.

"You're a real riot, Mick," Sal responded, sarcasm button firmly on.

"I guess I'd better text him back and RSVP for me and let him know that Johnny's out-of-town and might not be back," I said, but was cut off by another buzz from my phone.

"It's Johnny, he's replied already," I said as I stared at the screen. "He says he'll be there. That's great news, Helen must be feeling better."

CHAPTER 31

July 1st

"Here's a trivia question for you my friends," the secretly unhinged man with a lit unfiltered Camel cigarette in one hand and a box of popcorn in the other said as he shook a few of the tasty, fluffy kernels free down toward the hungry mouths of the badling of ducks congregated at his feet. "Outside of Manhattan where is the largest city park in New York located?"

"Give up? Look around you, you crazy quackers, you're in it – Hyde Park. I know, you'd think somewhere in Albany, Buffalo, Syracuse or Rochester, but you'd be wrong my fine feathered friends," Law said as he paused for a few puffs on what his Canadian friends quaintly referred to as a dart.

"We can thank good old Charles Hyde for that. He owned a paper company just over yonder on the corner of Pine Avenue and, what was then, Sugar Street," Law explained while using his index finger to point Southwest from where he was standing. "When he retired he bought a big tract of land right here and when he died of a stroke in 1921 his will revealed that he had left the land to the city for a public park to be built."

Law tapped out the smoke and placed it in a nearby trash can with the ducks waddling behind him all the while.

"Let's see where were we?" Law asked as he tossed more popcorn to his attentive audience.

"Oh yes, the park. So Hyde willed the land to kick start the project. Later, the Niagara Falls Power Company added another 58 acres to the kitty and one of the true jewels of our state was constructed. Look around you my fowl friends, there's the creek where you live, an Olympic-sized swimming pool, a Rose Garden, a golf course, baseball diamonds, tennis and bocce ball courts, a Veteran's Memorial, indoor ice skating rinks, volley-ball courts, a skateboarding park and a playground. Oh and that over there, Sal Maglie Stadium, that was built as a Works Progress Administration project during the Great Depression and was dedicated by none other than Franklin Delano Roosevelt himself. Impressive, I know."

Law shook out the ¼ box of remaining popcorn and took a moment to delight in the webbed-feet melee it caused.

"Back then people cared. Nobody even knows who Charles Hyde was these days. They think the park was named after the one in London. They should be throwing a parade for the man. The Greenway Commission should be honoring him and not a boat company that only went electric after a century plus of burning fossil fuels without so much as a second thought. Well, I bid you a fond adieu my friends, you are truly among the innocents," Law said as he walked away from the ducks and crossed the foot-bridge leading onto Duck Island.

Law sat on a bench and for a long time he just gazed at the slow-moving waters of Hyde Park Creek. He remembered coming to the sacred spot as a kid with his grandfather. He remembered the time as a child that he caught an 8 pound carp during the annual fishing derby right near the spot where he was now sitting. He'd been so excited to have his fish weighed before he set it free and was even more excited to find out that he'd won a trophy for 3rd place in his age bracket.

His mind was like a hummingbird, buzzing all over the place, but decisively in the past. He thought about the neighborhood in the city's North end that he grew up in. Times were so different then. The first school he'd attended, 22nd Street School, didn't even have a cafeteria. They actually let the kids out at noon everyday and Law and his classmates walked home for lunch. Law tried to imagine that happening today. Who would be there to greet the grade schoolers when they got home? Not mom, like it was in his day. Today's moms were either working two jobs or hitting the bottle or crack pipe once the kiddies headed out the door in the morning.

Law remembered those lunches, eating a Peanut Butter & Jelly sandwich and a warm bowl of Campbell's Chicken Noodle Soup while watching the Flintstones on a television that would be deemed tiny by today's standards. There were 3 generations in his home then. His grandparents lived upstairs in the split-level duplex, while Law and his baby sister lived with their parents downstairs. They were classified as lower middle class, but looking back on it Law realized they were rich by every measurable deemed important.

Law thought about the neighbors he had back then. Old lady Graff, who lived next door, was a kind soul that grew rhubarb behind her garage. Mr. Fitzgerald across the street was a shift worker who rented out one of the garages behind Law's house to park his car in inclement weather. The Gearys lived three doors down. They had 7 kids, the youngest of which was Law's age. Mrs. Richmond up the block used to give out pennies on Halloween and Law and his friends were delighted to receive them. She'd probably have them whipped back at her head by the kids that called that neighborhood home today, before they soaped her windows and poisoned her cat.

Everybody knew one another back then. Law remembered the time when he was a teenager and he talked back to Old Lady Graff when she had told him to keep his baseball from going into her yard. Mr. Fitzgerald happened to be arriving home from work and he grabbed Law by the scruff of his neck and made him apologize to the spinster. He then steered Law back home and knocked on the door and told Law's father what had transpired. Law's old man thanked Mr. Fitzgerald then commenced to give Law a beating in full view of the neighborhood. At the time Law hated his old man, but he'd give anything to be able to see him today and thank him for not sparing the rod on his behalf.

Law thought about the corner store everyone went to in that old neighborhood - Grobey's. Law's grandmother had an account there and she would send Law with a list of items to retrieve. Oftentimes, the list included a pack of filterless Camels for Law's grandfather. On those occasions, Law's grandmother would include a note giving her permission for the youngster to purchase the smokes. Grobey would take the note and toss the Camels into the bag with the other items after he'd marked the total down on an account that Law's grandmother would pay off at the beginning of each month.

As a reward for fetching the groceries, Law's grandmother would allow him to get $0.50 worth of candy from the store. Grobey stocked his store with the best candy in town. Law could often turn his allotted half dollar into a haul that included one giant pixie stick, one freezee pop, one box of lemon heads, five pretzel rods and 10 Swedish Fish. Man, those were the days.

But those days were so far gone in so many tangible ways. It was nothing more than disappearing vapors now. The houses in those neighborhoods still stood, but they were deteriorating fast. Hardly anyone owned his or her home these days. They were renters and they were transients. Absentee landlords were the norm. Kids were lucky if they knew their own daddy's name, let alone who the neighbors were. If a guy grabbed a misbehaving kid the way that Mr. Fitzgerald had back then, there would be no thank you from the child's parents. Instead, the interloper would get slapped in handcuffs and branded a child abuser and be ostracized from the neighborhood.

Times surely had changed, but for the better? Not by a long shot.

The end game is near, thought Law. *Really, this is the way that it always had to end. What would be the point in getting away with all of it, anyway? Infamy is the only type of fame worth anything when you come right down to it.*

It really couldn't have aligned any better, could it have? Governor Macy coming to town and acting like he gives a shit about this end of the state. And on the Niagara Falls Boat Ride to boot, talk about ending with an exclamation point. When I blow that floating tomato can sky high, with the Governor on board, that will make a statement that they'll have to listen to. Sadly, I'll go up with it, but if you don't have the stones you shouldn't be in the arena. I guess I'll know what it felt like to be one of those 9/11 hijackers. Allah got the glory and they got ripped apart by steel fragments part jetliner, part World Trade Center. Well, Mama never said being a martyr was easy.

The best part is that Mick O'Malley will be there with me. I'll have the distinct pleasure of seeing his horror-stricken face as the last thing I witness before I exit this God forsaken dimension.

Sweet salvation - I can hardly wait.

CHAPTER 32

It was the morning of July 3rd, also known as the busiest day of the year at Niagara Falls. Tomorrow would be Independence Day and most of the tourists at the Falls were enjoying a long weekend away from their normal drudgery. July 1st had been Canada Day and many inhabitants of that gentle nation were still milling about the falls trying to shake off the effects of one too many wobbly pops they'd imbibed while wishing Canada a happy birthday. The colliding of the two Independence Days always made July 3rd a day when people were squeezed close to the falls using plungers and Vaseline. This year was no exception and it was also the day that the Greenway Commission had chosen to pay tribute to the Niagara Falls Boat Ride. Oh, fucking joy.

It had been nearly 6 weeks since Law had begun his murderous spree. For 41 days my life had been turned upside down. Law had made me his puppet and had me dancing to his tune like a mindless court jester entertaining a spoiled king. Frankly, I was damned tired of it and I prayed to God Almighty nightly to let someone end his life before he saw another sunrise.

Sally had phoned me the night before to inform me that her captain had decided that she would better serve the protection detail if she was undercover. So she was headed over to pick me up and we would go as each other's date for the shindig.

I began dressing and started to slide into a two-piece suit before deciding to check the weather forecast for the day. A quick look at my app showed that they were calling for blue skies with a high of 90 degrees. I quickly changed course and went with a pair of breathable slacks topped with a short-sleeved dress shirt. A pair of casual Dockers Agent Bike Toe Slip On shoes rounded out the ensemble and I passed my own inspection in my hallway full-length mirror.

Sally arrived moments later looking resplendent in a cobalt blue summer dress with matching round-toe hollow-out flat sandals. She had a white Vera Wang purse slung over her shoulder, naturally it was perfectly contrasted to her outfit. Even though it was a date of necessity, I couldn't help but think that we made quite a fetching couple. I slid into the passenger seat of her Impala and was immediately thankful that the air conditioning was already nice and cold.

"How come you always drive us around?" I asked. "Why don't we take my wheels once in awhile?"

"What do you have against role reversal, Mick? Besides, I kind of like having a nice piece of eye candy like you riding shotgun. It's good for my image."

"Well, then feast your eyes, woman," I said as I pulled out a pair of Aviator sunglasses and slid them up the brim of my nose.

"You're a nut, Mick O'Malley. Your parents should have named you Macadamia. Hey, I've got something I've been meaning to throw at you, but I don't want you to go all apeshit on me."

"What is it, Sal? I promise to control my ingrained simian responses."

"I've been thinking about Law and why we can't figure out who the hell he is. We know that he's intelligent, we know that he's well-spoken. We know that he's principled and that he believes that he's protecting the integrity of the falls through his actions. We believe that because he uses you for his messages he must be American. We also believe that because his killings have happened on both sides of the border he must be a long time resident that has crossed the border many, many times."

"Sure, what are you getting at, Sal?" I asked.

"What if we can't find him because he's been hiding in plain sight? What if we don't see him because he's someone that you and I see, have seen, for most of our lives?"

"Who are you talking about, Sal?"

"John Brintkowski."

"No way," I laughed. "Professor Brintkowski? As Law?"

"Hear me out, Mick. He checks all of the boxes. Highly educated, fiercely articulate, American as apple pie with a close connection to you. He gives lectures in Canada often and he's in amazing shape for a man of his age. Didn't he compete in a triathlon last fall?"

"Yes, but we're talking about Professor Brintkowski here. A man of letters if ever I've met one." I protested.

"Exactly," Sally retorted. "And what's his greatest passion? The Greenway Commission. And what is at the heart of the Greenway Commission's purpose – to protect the integrity of Niagara Falls for generations to come."

I fell silent for a few minutes and Sally let me stew in my discontent while she steered her car into the state parking lot that led down to the boat docks.

"Jesus, Sal, I just can't imagine Professor Brintkowski killing anyone..." I said as my thought ran dry mid sentence.

"But?" Sally asked.

"But, something that he said at the Mayor's Ball just came back to me." I said.

"What was it, Mick?"

"He brought up Law and said that while his means were wrong his message was on point. That the Olmstead Vision that the Greenway Commission followed wasn't much different than what Law was preaching," I explained.

"So, I am on to something," Sally declared.

"That's not even the worst part, Sal. He then told me that Martin Luther King's pacifism was eventually pushed aside for Malcolm X's ideology. And he reminded me of the words that the Nation of Islam leader used to sell his message to the masses – 'By any means necessary.'"

CHAPTER 33

As Sally and I made our way off of the tower elevator that took us down to the Niagara Falls boats we were greeted with a scene atypical of Niagara Falls on a beautiful July afternoon. Tourists were being held at bay by the police as dignitaries were ushered toward the docked boat. However, before they could board they had to pass through a stricter security checkpoint than is found on most military bases.

First, there was a set of folding tables set up where the invited guests had to check in and provide two forms of trusted identification. Once they'd crossed that hurdle their names were checked off of the list and they were asked to remove their shoes and all metal items from their persons before they passed through an X-ray/metal detector not unlike the ones used by Homeland Security at the nation's top airports.

Finally, a member of Governor Macy's private detail went over them from head to toe with a security wand, taking the time to thoroughly frisk anyone that set off the sensor. I was happy that Sal's badge and my press credentials got us past all of those inconveniences.

Stepping aboard the ship it was like a who's who of Niagara Falls dignitaries. Mayor Thompson was front and center as were all of the members of his city council. His Canadian counterpart, Mayor Jay Beecher was present and I smiled as I saw that he was flanked by Ronnie Doyle. I noticed a few members from the county legislature in addition to our State Senator, George Fischer. My stomach began to turn when I noticed Jeffery Lordes hanging off of the VIP entourage like the parasite that he'd so obviously been reincarnated from.

Governor Macy then boarded, flanked by a six-member security detail. The two or three local TV stations that had sent reporters out to cover the ceremony began to roll video. The Governor began to press the flesh like he hadn't given one iota of thought to the lunatic that had captured the nation's attention all summer long.

Then I spotted him – Professor Brintkowski. He was in a small group of people all associated with the Greenway Commission. He was impeccably dressed in a three-piece tailored suit and his silver hair was styled just so with Brylcreem. I gave him a once over with my eyes and for the first time noticed that he was quite powerfully built for a man of his advanced years. Sal was right, he'd have no problem taking down most men half his age.

"Hey, Mick, Sal what's happening?"

I turned and was surprised to see Johnny Guts at my shoulder. He was wearing long pants and one of the *Insider* windbreakers we'd decided to purchase last spring.

"Hey, John. Helen must be doing better I take it?" I asked.

"Yeah, she's tougher than a $2.00 steak I'll tell you. She wanted to wait on me, can you believe that one, Mick?"

"For her? Yeah, I can believe it. When did you get back in town?" I asked.

"About an hour ago. I got up at the ass crack of dawn and hit the 90," Johnny responded.

"What's with the windbreaker, Johnny? You expecting a cold front we don't know about," Sally asked him.

"Ha-ha, no. I left my press card at mom's house, this was the only thing that kept me out of that Orwellian line-up to get on the boat," Johnny explained.

"Ah, gotcha," Sally said, but was cut off as John Brintkowski stepped up to a podium and began speaking.

"If I may have everyone's attention please," Brintkowski began. "My name is John Brintkowski and I am delighted that you could all make it here today on this momentous occasion."

I touched Johnny Guts on the shoulder and gave a nod goodbye as Sal and I slowly made our way through the crowd for a closer view. For the first time, I noticed a uniformed Darnell Morgan among the line of officers that flanked either side of the podium. He was standing closest to Brintkowski on his left hand side. Like the other officers with him, he was wearing protective body armor.

"Keep your eyes on Brintkowski and watch for any sudden or unnatural movements," Sal whispered as we got to within 10 feet of where the professor was standing.

Despite my disbelief that he could really be evil I found myself staring at him like a hungry dog staring at a hambone on the other side of a chain link fence.

"It is my great honor to stand before you as, on behalf of the Greenway Commission, we bestow our esteemed President's Green Medal of Honor on the good people of the Niagara Falls Boat Ride Company," Brintkowski said as the crowd erupted in respectful applause.

"On this day, the Niagara Falls Boat Ride Company is debuting its new fleet of all-electric boats, making it the most Earth-friendly attraction in the entire nation."

More applause followed as my brain tried to recollect something that I just couldn't bring to the surface.

"As you all know, this has been the most trying summer in our history. Yet, we must not let the message be spoiled by the methodology of the messenger. The Olmstead vision is the only right one for Niagara Falls and today we embrace the ways that it can be incorporated into this century and in going forward," Brintkowski said as TV cameras rolled and cameras flashed.

"Now, it is my great pleasure to introduce to you our forward-thinking leader of New York State, Governor Macy."

Heavy applause ensued as Brintkowski shook the governor's hand and slid over to stand at his left shoulder. The feeling of a thought that was begging to be remembered once again rose within me. What was it? Damn it! I knew that it was a missing piece of the puzzle that had eluded us for so long, but what was it?

Sally touched me on the arm and motioned that she was going to flank out to get a view of Brintkowski from another angle.

"Thank you Professor Brintkowski. The Greenway Commission, Senator Fischer, Mayors Thompson and Beecher, the staff of the Niagara Falls Boat Ride Company and all other dignitaries and attendees, welcome. We gather today to celebrate one of New York's oldest and most cherished companies as they enter a new chapter, one that sees them leading the way as we move away from our dependence on fossil fuels and toward a cleaner, more earth-friendly alternative. The all-electric boats that we christen today will become the industry-standard for tomorrow and all days going forward," Governor Macy said to wild applause.

As if on cue the boat's engines fired on and it pulled away for a celebratory cruise up to the base of the falls.

"I know that the people of Niagara Falls, as well as all New Yorkers, have been through a trying time unprecedented in our history. Let today, and the good news it brings, be a message of healing and a harbinger of good things to come."

As the Governor spoke, I saw Brintkowski reach into his inside breast pocket. In the split second that it took for his hand to disappear it hit me – the missing piece of the puzzle that had eluded me for so long.

Johnny's tattoo, Johnny's goddamned tattoo! Olmstead, the man that had inspired the Olmstead vision so often referenced by Brintkowski and the Greenway Commission. But, just as importantly his was the name taken by the man that had stolen so many lives in the name of his misguided crusade. Olmstead, the 19th century American landscape architect, journalist, social critic, and public administrator. The man that designed Central Park in New York City, Prospect Park in Brooklyn and Cadwalader Park in Trenton, New Jersey among many others. He was also the man that was invited to study Niagara Falls in the 1880s and after doing so declared that nothing need be changed about the park surrounding the falls, save that it needed to be preserved just as it was – natural and true to God's plan.

Thus the Olmstead vision was born. But it was his name, his full name that came back to me now and filled me with an immediate and simultaneous sense of knowing and horror. Frederick Law Olmsted. His middle name was Law! It was there all along and Johnny had placed his likeness on his body in indelible ink as a clue to mock me and I'd failed to see it.

Brintkowski's hand emerged from his pocket clutching something metallic. I glanced over and saw Sally pull her service revolver from her purse.

"Noooo," I screamed as a shot rang out on the boat's deck.

Only it wasn't from Sally's gun.

"Get down," I heard Darnell Morgan scream as a second shot immediately followed the first.

Morgan dove in front of Governor Macy and was struck by two

bullets. The first hit his well-protected chest. The second, however, lodged at just the right spot where there was a gap in his armor at his shoulder. It severed a vital artery, sending a geyser of blood flowing into the humid air. The Governor hit the deck as his security detail covered his body and drew their weapons. Professor Brintkowski stood stunned, clutching the silver pocket watch he'd retrieved from his breast pocket.

I lunged forward and fell to the ground next to the fallen Darnell Morgan.

"O'Malley," he said to me as blood poured from his mouth. "Tell Ayesha I love her."

Those were his final words as Darnell Morgan, who had spent the majority of his professional life as a villain, died a hero.

CHAPTER 34

Have you ever noticed that in times of great danger everything begins moving in slow motion? It's one of humanities great defense mechanisms as it gives our brains time to process all that is happening and take the best course of action to ensure our survival. I was in that mode now as all hell was breaking loose everywhere around me.

I looked down and saw Darnell Morgan's eyes glaze over as the last vestiges of life left his body along with his soul. I could hear the Governor's security detail asking if he was okay and barking out orders to secure the perimeter. I saw Sally standing over me, service revolver in her extended right hand, and heard her ask me if I was okay. I nodded in the affirmative.

"And Morgan?" She asked.

"He's gone," I managed to mumble before adding, "Johnny, Johnny."

"He's somewhere over there," Sally motioned, not understanding that I was trying to tell her the identity of the shooter.

All of this was happening against a backdrop of pure bedlam. The crowd was in a state of panic as they were screaming and trying to figure a way off of the boat despite the fact that it had left the dock and was a good 50-yards from shore.

Just then another shot rang out, silencing everyone.

Johnny Guts stepped forward, his windbreaker was open revealing a torso completely wrapped with plastic explosives. In his left hand was a detonator with the plunger fully compressed. He had a Ruger LCP in his right hand and he spoke directly to the Governor's Security Detail and the officers of the Niagara Falls Police Department, all of which had their weapons trained directly at him.

"Easy now gentlemen. If I let go of this plunger we all will be blown higher than Willie Nelson on 4/20. Let me formally introduce myself, many of you know me as Johnny Gutanzarro, but that is more of what you might call my not-so-secret identity. I prefer to be known by my alter-ego. You find yourselves graced with the presence of the one, the only, Law."

A collective gasp went up from the crowd. I stole a glance at Sally and saw a wave of recognition roll across her face at what I had been trying to tell her. I also noticed that she slipped her gun back into her purse.

"Now, I am going to ask you all to kindly toss your weapons into the river," Johnny/Law requested.

No one immediately responded. Law fired another shot straight up into the air.

"I'm afraid that I am going to have to insist. I've never been a fan of baseball, so in this case it's two strikes and you're out. If I have to ask again I'll let go of this plunger and you'd all better hope that heaven doesn't have the 'No Vacancy' sign lit."

"Do what he says," Governor Macy, who had gotten back to his feet, ordered. "I don't want anyone else dead on account of this man."

"Ah, and people say that you just can't elect capable leadership these days," Law said. "You heard the man, I want those guns overboard and I want it done right now."

Reluctantly, the assemblage of protectors complied. Plunk after plunk could be heard as one metal peacekeeper after another was tossed overboard and sunk to the bottom of the Niagara River. Sally made no move to open her purse.

"Wonderful, now..." Law began, but was cut off by Governor Macy.

"What exactly do you want from us?" the Governor demanded

Law stepped forward and clipped him in the mouth with the butt of his pistol, drawing blood.

The crowd gasped and the security detail flexed, but no one made a move.

"You do not question me, do you understand? I am running the show and I will ask the questions and divulge only what I damn well please. Do I make myself clear?" Law stated.

Ronnie Doyle tensed up as if he was thinking about rushing Law, but Sally caught his eye and slowly shook her head no.

"You folks from the TV networks, I'll kindly ask you to keep rolling video. There's much that we need to cover and I'd like as big of an audience as we can get. Mick, would you please step forward and stand next to the Governor?" Law instructed.

Hearing my name shook things out of slow motion and I could feel my heart beating at hyper speed through my chest cavity. I felt my feet begin to shuffle and I made my way forward to the spot he had specified.

"What do I want from you, that's what you wanted to know isn't it Governor? Well, it's a loaded question and seeing as how I am the only loaded one left on this boat," Law said as he looked down at the plastic explosives and laughed out loud, "I am going to grace you with an answer."

Law then tossed his gun into the river.

"No need for this anymore. Kind of like bringing a sandwich to a picnic, eh?" he said as he once again looked down at the deadly amount of explosives adhered to his body.

Law then pulled a pack of filterless Camels from his coat pocket and adroitly shook one to his lips using only his right hand. He then threw the pack down on the ship's deck before extracting a lighter and turning the tip of the cigarette bright orange.

"Seems like a good day to quit smoking. Nasty habit, I think this will be my last. What do I want from you? That was the question, yes? Well, gather round boys and girls and I will tell you exactly what I demand from all of you."

CHAPTER 35

"Let me tell you all a little story," Law began as he took a long drag on the Camel for dramatic effect. "Once upon a time two men met in a bar and decided to start a newspaper."

Law paused for a moment and looked over his captive, pun intended, audience and seemed to take glee in their full attention.

"These two men, oh let's call them Mick and Johnny for shits and giggles, shall we? These two men decided to start this newspaper because they wanted to affect change in Niagara Falls. They felt that the daily rag was a waste of ink and paper – offense intended Lordes – and that they could offer the citizenry something more substantive. They agreed that their newspaper would answer to a higher calling. That it would, 'Comfort the afflicted and afflict the comfortable.' Do you remember that, Mick?"

"Yeah, I remember, Johnny," I said.

"Johnny's dead, Mick. Been dead for a long time. Refer to me as Law or I'll have them throw you into the river at the base of the falls where it's 150-feet deep. Do you understand me?"

"Sure, Law. Whatever you say," I said, though I couldn't quite hide the sarcasm in my cadence.

"So to continue with our trip down memory lane, we threw caution to the wind and we started the *Insider*. We agreed that we would write stories that exposed greed and corruption. We targeted the chemical dumping at Niagara Falls as an area that we would expose and get to the truth. We said that over commercialization was nearly as bad. We said, Mick, that we didn't own the falls at Niagara, that we had simply borrowed them from our children and that we were honor bound to turn them over to the next generation in better shape than they had been handed to us. Do you fucking remember that, Mick?" Law screamed in my face.

"I remember," I said.

"Oh, so you remember, but you have just chosen to piss all over those sentiments, is that it Mick?" Law said as he, presumably for the first time, took notice of Darnell Morgan's dead body lying mere feet in front of him. "Oh, for fuck's sake somebody take his body and toss it overboard, will you?"

"He was a police officer with a family, Joh, er Law. You can't throw his body into the river," I protested.

"Mick, Mick, Mick, this is me you're talking to here. I now how much you hated that son-of-a-bitch. I didn't plan on filling him with lead today, those bad boys were meant for Mr. Governor here, but 'You're welcome, Mick. No extra charge,'" Law taunted. "Now, throw his worthless carcass to the fishes."

"I can't let you do that, Sir," Ronnie Doyle said, stepping forward. "Please have the decency to let me and one of the officers move his body to the back of the boat so that he may have a proper funeral."

"Proper funeral? Jesus, you Canadians are so damned righteous. Fine, if it makes you feel better move his body to the back of the boat and he can become fish food with the rest of you when I blow us all up," Law said.

Ronnie Doyle and Darnell Morgan's partner, Charlie Whitehurst, picked up his lifeless form and shuffled him to the rear of the deck.

"Now where were we? Oh yes, we launch a paper with lofty intentions, but it soon goes off track doesn't it, Mick? You see, my erstwhile partner here was too busy shagging his little college girlfriend and spending his money on whatever shiny bauble caught her eye to do anything more than chase ad revenue. The stories that we wanted to expose all remained hidden. We forgot to afflict the comfortable, instead we used the afflicted to become comfortable."

"Johnny, I don't know what to say," I said before Law cut me off.

"I said that Johnny is dead! That's your problem, Mick, you only hear what you want to. You only listen to your dick. We had a chance to make this city relevant again. We had an opportunity to give voice to the voiceless, to avenge the wronged, to - as the President is fond of saying - drain the swamp of all of the elitist bastards that have gotten fat in Niagara Falls while generations of poor have gone hungry."

Law paused to let his words sink in for dramatic effect. As he stared up into the midday sun organizing his thoughts, I saw Sally slowly slide her revolver out of her purse and begin to inch herself ever closer along the aft side of the boat.

"You're garbage, Mick. You're almost worse than the others because you had enough sense to see how badly this city needed a hero, you just didn't have the guts to be one. But, you're hardly the only one at fault here. Governor Macy, you didn't think that I'd forgotten about you, did you?"

The Governor, still smarting from the smack to the mouth he'd received, decided that there was no end game in verbally responding to his captor, so he simply shook his head no.

"I must say that it is nice to see you at this end of the state. I know we're the redheaded stepchildren of New York. I mean, we can't carry an election. What New York City wants, New York City gets, am I right?"

This time the Governor nodded in the affirmative.

"For the record, by the way, this is Western New York, not up-state or downstate or whatever incorrect qualifier you Albany assholes label us with. I'm sure I speak for all of us when I say we hope you and everyone in the Big Apple would just secede and leave us the fuck alone. Am I right people?" Law asked.

No one said a word.

"They're just scared shitless, otherwise they'd be chanting like Gregorian Monks. You, Governor Macy, you have a deplorable record of support for Niagara Falls. I mean, come on, it's only one of the top tourist destinations in America. Natural Wonder of the World and all that jazz. It's on your fucking license plate for Chrissakes. But, what have you done to help us here, Governor? What?"

Sal inched a bit closer. She wasn't looking my way at all, but it was like I could feel her thoughts. I knew that she was about to make a move and, instinctively, I knew what my role was in her plan.

"You, and the men that sat in the chair before you, sent chemicals here to pollute our land and corrupt our drinking water. You sentenced our children to lives cut short by tumors and cancer. You took one of God's greatest gifts and you shit all over it," Law said as his face turned bright red with rage.

Get ready, Mick I could feel Sally telling me telepathically. *This is no time to punt, be a hero.*

"What do I want from you, Governor? What do I want from all of you?" Law said as he raised his left hand, the one holding the plunger down, up over his head. "I want you to die. I want you all to be martyrs. Your deaths here today will send a message that Niagara Falls must be respected. Take heart you unfortunate puppets, you will not die in vain. You will be remembered as the sacrifices that woke up the Gods behind the waterfalls. And now we must say adieu. It is time to…"

Now! I could feel Sally command.

I leapt forward and grabbed onto Johnny's hand. I jammed my thumb down over his and exerted all of my might. At the same moment, Sally aimed her revolver and sent a bullet into the far depths of Law's skull. He was dead before his body hit the boat deck. I went to the ground with him. There was screaming everywhere as people aboard readied to meet St. Peter.

That day would have to wait because my thumb was firmly over Johnny's and there was no way that I was letting go until a bomb squad said I could.

CHAPTER 36

July 11th

I sat alone at a park bench that flanked the bustling upper rapids just above the American Falls. Sally was due to join me in about 15 minutes, so I had a bit of quiet time to collect my thoughts.

So much had happened since that fateful day on the Niagara Falls Boat Ride. I'd held the plunger down on that detonator for nearly 2 ½ hours in the blazing dog days of summer sun before the bomb squad was able to get to us and get it defused. All the while I was lying on top of my best friend and my business partner. A guy that I would have sworn that I knew like the back of my hand, but now realized that I never knew him, the real him, from Adam.

Governor Macy was whisked off to safety by his security detail. Not before he profusely thanked both Sally and I for saving his life. I guess the severity of the moment caused him to temporarily lose sight of the fact that there were over 300 other folks on board that had also narrowly escaped an early check-out from Hotel Life. Five days later, he called a hastily organized press conference and announced his immediate retirement from office. He said that the close call made him reevaluate his choices and he had come to the conclusion that time with his wife and children was his new top priority.

Special Agent Carlson held another press conference and once again stated that the FBI was closing the case on Law. This time everyone believed him. He said that Law's death and the thwarting of his plan to blow up the Niagara Falls Boat Ride would begin the healing process for the families of all of his victims. Amen to that.

The live video of Law's speech on the boat deck and of his death and the bomb squad aftermath that the local TV stations had captured had been viewed by hundreds of millions world wide. As a result I'd become as famous as Mohammad Ali at his apex and I had taken to not stepping out in public without sporting dark sunglasses and a ball cap.

A funeral was held for Darnell Morgan where he was lauded as a hero who had saved the life of Governor Macy. Sally and I attended as did some 8,000 others. Officers from police departments as far away as Ohio were on hand, all in uniform. Manuela and Ayesha sat front row, dressed in black and they both wept heavily for the husband and father that had let them both down. I think they also wept for the redeemed man that might have emerged had fate not had other designs.

Sally and I had appeared on just about every news show from coast to coast. Most via satellite, but we had been flown out to New York and Washington, DC. I admired how well she handled herself in front of a camera, almost as well as she did at the business end of a revolver. We were the toast of America and I'd never felt closer to her.

Next week we were headed back to Washington where we were going to be awarded the Presidential Medal of Freedom at a White House ceremony. I couldn't believe it. It still all felt like some surreal dream. Jesus, my mom sure was the queen of her Words with Friends circle these days, that was for sure.

Just then a family with two young girls walked by on the path in front of me. They were headed to Prospect Point and a front row view of the falls.

"Are the Niagara Falls just up ahead, Mommy?" the youngest, about four, asked.

"Yes, they are sweetheart. Just a bit farther," her mother replied.

"I can't wait," the little girl said. "I bet they're more beautiful than a thousand unicorns looking at a thousand rainbows."

"I bet they are, too," her mother said, laughing.

I caught myself laughing, too. *Man, we really don't own them, do we? We are honor bound to turn them over to the children in better shape than we'd found them. Johnny had that much right anyway,* I thought.

"Hey, handsome. Is this seat taken?"

I snapped out of my meditative state to see that Sally had arrived right on schedule.

"I was saving it for the most famous ginger since Ann Margaret, but until she gets here, go ahead," I joked.

"Don't you think you look more conspicuous in that getup, Mick?" Sally asked.

"Nobody has bothered me yet today," I said as I took off the shades. Then, as if on cue, a young Hispanic couple strolled by and did a double take.

"It's you, isn't it? the female queried. "You're the two that got Law."

"No, we're from California," Sal bluffed.

"No you ain't," her boyfriend countered. "You're them. Holy shit. Hey, can we get a selfie?"

Before I could properly protest, he'd fished his phone out of his pocket and quickly moved himself and his lady love into position before snapping off a shot earmarked for social media.

"Thanks," he said as he checked to make sure the pic met with his approval. "You guys are the bomb."

As the two of them made their way off, Sal and I looked at each other and both of us burst out laughing.

"I guess that's the new reality," Sal said.

"Yeah, I guess it is. Are you ready for the Washington trip?" I asked.

"Just about. Craig officially moved out and signed the divorce petition so that's made things easier. The kids are doing okay, all things considered. How about you, Mick? What are your plans going forward?"

"Well, I reached out to Lisa Wilson. I told her that I'd like to become a full time volunteer with the teen group. I don't know, Sal, but as crazy as he was, Johnny was right that we need to put the kids first."

"That's great, Mick. Maybe I'll join you. I've been thinking that I should be giving more back to the community."

"I would love that, Sal. Also, the owners of the Niagara Falls Boat Ride reached out to me yesterday. They wanted to offer me a cash reward for saving their expensive boat. I told them they could honor me by paying for Ayesha Morgan's college expenses. They agreed and will announce it tomorrow."

"Mick, that's fabulous. Look at you, you're getting really good at this adulting business."

"Better late than never," I responded.

"What about the *Insider?* What's the future of the paper going to be?" Sally asked.

"I don't know, but it's going to be different. I do want to get back to what our original intentions were. I want to give a voice to the downtrodden. I want to expose corruption. I want to make a goddamned difference. Or die trying. What about you, Sal? What do you want from the future?"

"I'm glad that you asked, Mr. O'Malley. I can't speak for the entirety of the future, but I can tell you want I want right now."

"And what's that?" I asked.

"Well, even though I am not officially divorced I would like to be taken out on a good old fashioned date. Flowers, movie, dinner – the whole nine yards. Might you be so inclined as to be my paramour, Mick?"

In the few seconds that it took me to respond a whole encyclopedia of thoughts raced through my mind. Chief amongst them was this thought: You know how people always say that things happen for a reason? Even though in most cases it's just a defense mechanism to get them through a difficult time? This was not that. All of the crazy and unprecedented events that had transpired at Niagara Falls over the summer had happened for a reason. They had changed and transformed both Sal and I and they had led us right here to this moment in time.

So I decided to answer her question with action. I kissed her. Long and hard and deep and she kissed me back with the same passion. I drank in the strawberry taste of her lips. I got lost in the gentle rhythm of her breathing. My hand went to her hair and it felt like crimson silk. When finally our lips parted I looked hard into her eyes and I saw something clearly represented there – our future. It was sunny and bright and full of endless possibilities. It was as far from darkness as one could hope to be and I couldn't wait to explore every inch of it with her hand in mine.

"I'd be honored to be your date, Sal. I thought you'd never ask."

THE END

ACKNOWLEDGE-MENTS

When it comes to writing a novel the old African proverb has it right – it takes a village. To have these characters, which began as a small germ in my head, come to fruition and transform into fully formed entities is something that I had a lot of help in realizing.

My brother-in-law, Niagara Falls Police Lieutenant David Cudahy, was an invaluable resource in bringing Sally Wendt properly to the page. His insights into the inner workings of a police department, the terminology used and the interactions between different levels of law enforcement provided Sally with an authenticity she would have otherwise lacked.

Dean Kindig and I are Buffalo Bills brothers in arms. When I first became aware of Dean's stellar writing recapping events at the Bills' training camp facilities at St. John Fisher College I knew he possessed a tailored ability to craft words that just can't be bought off the rack.

Once we became familiar with one another I began describing Dean with a line I once heard Neil Young casually toss out, "We're old friends that have only just met."

Dean's 45 year career as an educator in the Pittsford and Brighton school districts has provided him with an impressive command of the English language. His proofreads were so helpful in reeling in my propensity for playing loose and fast with the

Queen's English. I'm sure there are still a few too many preposi-
tions and too few Harvard commas for Dean's liking, but you
would have shuddered at the rough draft.

Thanks for taking on one more student in your illustrious career, Dean.

I first met Robert Hookey nearly 20 years ago when I accepted a
job to be the Director of Tourism for the Hilton Fallsview Hotel.
Someone had told him that I was a big Marvel and DC comics
fan in my youth. He walked up to me and handed me an Aven-
gers comic and, in his best impersonation of a drug dealer, said,
"Here, if this hits you the right way, you know where to find me."
We've been thick as thieves ever since.

He was the first to read the finished script and his support, con-
structive criticism and artistic suggestions are both welcomed
and appreciated.

Robert makes a cameo in Chapter 18 and in the praise section
that precedes the first chapter. While all of the characters in
Niagara Falls Into Darkness are fictitious "The Hook" is, as Ri-
hanna is wont to say, as real as you and me. He is a crackerjack
bellman who also happens to be a published author and a popu-
lar blogger. Google him and follow his writing exploits – you
won't regret it.

Kenny Levy has been my best buddy for a long time. He is the
most fiercely articulate person I have ever met and has an appe-
tite to devour literature unmatched in the Tri-State area.

I have borrowed some of his most colorful phrases and put them
into the mouths of my protagonist and antagonist. The book is
far better for it, just like I am a far better man for having his en-
dearing friendship. Thanks, homie.

I not only married a beautiful woman, but I married a brilliant
one as well. My wife, Maureen, is not only my confidante and
muse, but her many years in the medical profession proved to

be invaluable in the scenes involving Manuela and Ayesha Morgan.

Oh, and like Sally Wendt she is a stunning Ginger. Art reflecting life? You betcha.

Thank you dear for always being the better part of me. I don't know how I got so lucky.

Lastly, there is a ghost haunting the pages of *NFID*. I had the life-altering good fortune to have spent 13 years as a feature columnist for the original *Niagara Falls Reporter*. I wrote under the tutelage of the late Mike Hudson.

Mike was punk rock royalty as the founder of the pioneering group *The Pagans*. He took on a second career in journalism and co-founded a weekly newspaper that forever altered the course of that medium in Niagara Falls.

I didn't base Mick O'Malley on Mike Hudson, but I gave him Mike's moxie and some of his attributes. I also gave him Mike's Irish heritage – it just felt right. Mike's spirit inhabits these pages and I'd like to think that would bring a smile to his face.

Mike Hudson was a complex individual and my relationship with him, like all of his relationships, was bittersweet. But I wouldn't trade it for the world. RIP, my friend.

Made in the USA
Las Vegas, NV
17 July 2021